I didn't see the feet until I ran into the man. I plunged into him full force and he stepped back with the impact and threw a steadying arm around me.

I looked up and nearly screamed. "Damian!"

"Chloe, are you all right?"

"I was just getting out of the storm," I said, trying not to let him hear the fear in my voice.

"You shouldn't be out here alone."

I was dripping but no longer being pelted with rain. Instead, I was pressed against his broad chest under his umbrella. I was too aware of this man of whom I needed to be suspicious. I couldn't trust anyone until I knew the truth.

"There's a horse out there." I glanced back the way I had come. "A gray Thoroughbred."

Damian laughed at me. "You have quite an imagination. The only pale horse on this estate was a gray stud that died in a terrible fall off the bluffs last month."

Goose bumps prickled up my spine. "What about a neighbor's horse?"

"There are no other grays." He placed a hand intimately on the small of my back to lead me back to the house, then added mockingly, "You must have seen a ghost horse."

Dear Harlequin Intrigue Reader,

This July, Intrigue brings you six sizzling summer reads. They're the perfect beach accessory.

* We have three fantastic miniseries for you. *Film at Eleven* continues THE LANDRY BROTHERS by Kelsey Roberts. Gayle Wilson is back with the PHOENIX BROTHERHOOD in *Take No Prisoners.* And B.J. Daniels finishes up her McCALLS' MONTANA series with *Shotgun Surrender.*

* Susan Peterson brings you *Hard Evidence,* the final installment in our LIPSTICK LTD. promotion featuring stealthy sleuths. And, of course, we have a spine-tingling ECLIPSE title. This month's is Patricia Rosemoor's *Ghost Horse.*

* Don't miss Dana Marton's sexy stand-alone title, *The Sheik's Safety.* When an American soldier is caught behind enemy lines, she'll fake amnesia to guard her safety, but there's no stopping the sheik determined on winning her heart.

Enjoy our stellar lineup this month and every month!

Sincerely,

Denise O'Sullivan
Senior Editor
Harlequin Intrigue

PATRICIA ROSEMOOR

GHOST HORSE

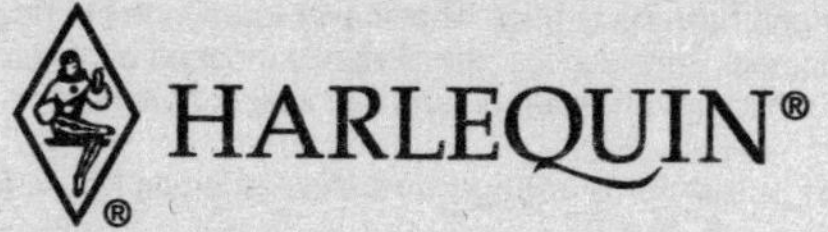

TORONTO • NEW YORK • LONDON
AMSTERDAM • PARIS • SYDNEY • HAMBURG
STOCKHOLM • ATHENS • TOKYO • MILAN • MADRID
PRAGUE • WARSAW • BUDAPEST • AUCKLAND

If you purchased this book without a cover you should be aware that this book is stolen property. It was reported as "unsold and destroyed" to the publisher, and neither the author nor the publisher has received any payment for this "stripped book."

ISBN 0-373-22858-9

GHOST HORSE

This edition published by arrangement with Harlequin Books S.A.

www.eHarlequin.com

Printed in U.S.A.

ABOUT THE AUTHOR

"Dangerous love" always fascinated Patricia Rosemoor ever since she started watching erotic thriller movies—a fascination she has brought into her work. She's written more Harlequin Intrigue books than any other author. She also writes for Harlequin Blaze and Silhouette Bombshell, bringing a different mix of thrills and chills to each line. She's won a Golden Heart from Romance Writers of America and Reviewers Choice and Career Achievement Awards from the *Romantic Times* Book Club.

Contact Patricia via e-mail—
Patricia@PatriciaRosemoor.com or snail mail,
Patricia Rosemoor, Harlequin Books, 233 Broadway,
New York, NY 10279. Check out her Web site
www.PatriciaRosemoor.com.

Books by Patricia Rosemoor

HARLEQUIN INTRIGUE

38—DOUBLE IMAGES
55—DANGEROUS ILLUSIONS
74—DEATH SPIRAL
81—CRIMSON HOLIDAY
95—AMBUSHED
113—DO UNTO OTHERS
121—TICKET TO NOWHERE
161—PUSHED TO THE LIMIT
163—SQUARING ACCOUNTS
165—NO HOLDS BARRED
199—THE KISS OF DEATH
219—TORCH JOB
243—DEAD HEAT
250—HAUNTED
283—SILENT SEA
291—CRIMSON NIGHTMARE
317—DROP DEAD GORGEOUS
346—THE DESPERADO
361—LUCKY DEVIL
382—SEE ME IN YOUR DREAMS*
386—TELL ME NO LIES*
390—TOUCH ME IN THE DARK*
439—BEFORE THE FALL
451—AFTER THE DARK
483—NEVER CRY WOLF*
499—A LOVER AWAITS
530—COWBOY JUSTICE
559—HEART OF A LAWMAN†
563—THE LONE WOLF'S CHILD†
567—A RANCHER'S VOW†
629—SOMEONE TO PROTECT HER
661—MYSTERIOUS STRANGER*
665—COWBOY PROTECTOR*
684—GYPSY MAGIC
"Andrei"
703—FAKE I.D. WIFE**
707—VIP PROTECTOR**
745—THE BOYS IN BLUE
"Zachary"
785—VELVET ROPES**
791—ON THE LIST**
858—GHOST HORSE

SILHOUETTE BOMBSHELL

24—HOT CASE

*The McKenna Legacy
†Sons of Silver Springs
**Club Undercover

CAST OF CHARACTERS

Chloe Morgan—The summer tutor came to Graylord Pastures wanting to know the fate of her friend, not to fall in love with her employer.

Damian Graylord—The dark and brooding master of the estate seemed more interested in getting close to Chloe than he did about Dawn's disappearance.

Dawn Reed—Why would Chloe's best friend not tell her she meant to elope with some mysterious man…and then vanish?

Alex Graylord—Damian's amiable and talkative brother wants out of the family business, but at what cost?

Nissa Graylord—Does Damian's thirteen-year-old daughter have clues to what happened to Dawn?

Priscilla Graylord—The ex-Mrs. Graylord disappeared in the night, but is she haunting the estate?

Mrs. Avery—What secrets did the housekeeper hired by Priscilla keep?

Theo Bosch—Did the barn manager resent Damian enough to try to ruin him?

Clifford Wakeley—Was the horse groom who acted like the world owed him something getting revenge for his brother…or himself?

Jack Larson—What would the Graylords' neighbor do to get the farm he so desperately wanted?

Prologue

Thunder rumbled in the distance, signaling another storm rolling in. Thick fog, as if sent to make the task more difficult, rose from the Mississippi River and up the jagged bluffs. It was hard enough for the watcher to do what was necessary in the dark and without the moon, only the flashlight allowed one to see what was what.

The watcher swept a beam of light across the pale gray hide. "C'mon, Centaur, there you go, now." The soft words were meant to deceive this cleverest of beasts.

Even so, the stallion seemed to sense no good would come of this night. He whinnied and snorted and danced through muck and across rain-slippery rock, away from the one who led him. Biting down impatience, the human let out some more line to avoid a struggle.

Damn horse was stubborn. If he got it in his head to bolt too soon…

"Attaboy, nice and easy now."

The soft reassurance seemed to calm the beast. Now to inch closer to the bluffs. The lead went taut when the horse didn't follow. A low whistle made his ears twitch, and after a moment of hesitation, Centaur bobbed his head and the taut connection weakened.

The beast in all his glory stepped through the fog into the light, instilling the watcher with enormous regret. Such raw beauty. A refined head with widely spaced, intelligent eyes. Its pale mane fluttered between those pools of dark liquid now focused on him. A bit sick inside, the human looked away and took a deep breath and considered the options.

No! This was the best one.

The weapon slid free of the belt loop as they circled a bit, the stallion prancing closer to the bluff.

The bridle had to go now. "I'm sorry it has to be this way, boy, I really am."

The regret was punctuated with a blast of the air horn, which if heard, would seem to come from a boat on the river. The stallion's head immediately shot up, and his eyes rolled white. Another blast and the stallion danced away, muscles bunching, hooves doing a nervous tap dance on the wet rocks. The third blast, backed by rolling thunder, was the charm.

Lightning crackled and the pale stallion glowed eerily against the fog as it reared. A hoof smacked the noisemaker out of the gloved hand. The jarring movement twisted the horse's big body, and his hooves slipped on wet rock. Panicked, Centaur threw up his head and danced sideways. Suddenly he seemed to slip and his rear quarters went down, then disappeared from sight. The horse screamed and screamed as he tried to regain footing.

A losing battle….

Suddenly the horse's head plunged backward, his body following in a bizarre slow-motion dance over the cliff and into the mists. The fog muffled the sounds of his struggle as he plummeted to certain death on the rocks below.

But wait…a scream was still coming from somewhere…from the opposite direction…this one human.

A glance back as lightning struck once more, and the figure at the edge of the woods was illuminated.

She'd witnessed everything….

Chapter One

As I drove through fog as thick as soup along switchback curves that took me through the hilly northwestern corner of Illinois, I asked myself if I knew what I was doing. Every so often, when I thought about it, my skin crawled or my stomach knotted or I had trouble swallowing.

Fear was my constant companion, one I hadn't shed since setting out alone from Chicago several hours ago in my used car I'd bought on my meager teacher's salary. I told myself that I was not being foolish or reckless. That I was doing what I must.

That Dawn would do the same for me.

Only, part of me was willing to admit that maybe she wouldn't. There was a selfish part of the young woman who was my best friend and the closest thing I had to a sister that I didn't want to recognize.

I left the curves and the fog behind and eventually saw the sign to Galena, but I turned away from the old town that had once grown rich on mining. I headed south, toward Savanna, and as I traveled, I knew I was getting closer to the Mississippi River. Excitement mingled with apprehension for a moment. I'd never been this far from Chicago before.

An unexpected sense of adventure reared its head and for a few moments I coasted on the newness of the area, on the freshness of the air wafting through my open car window.

But not today, I thought, as a sign reminded me of why I was here: Graylord Pastures.

I turned onto the Thoroughbred horse farm and drove between limestone pillars, which provided the framework for an iron gate that lay open, as if in welcome. But I felt no welcome here. Only dread. Not being deceitful by nature, I hoped I could pull this off.

The drive curved around and upward, and at its end I saw the gray stone wreathed in curlicues of fog as if the house itself was rising from the mists. Not a house really—more like a ghostly mansion, three stories with mostly arched windows, though no pair was identical with any other pair. From the size and height of the house, I guessed it had more than a dozen rooms all with high ceilings and, judging by the bizarre placement of chimneys of different widths and heights, multiple fireplaces. It was a century-old house, and undoubtedly those fireplaces had once been the building's only source of heat.

As I drew closer, I passed an old gazebo not far from the house itself and overlooking both barns and pasture. Two men conferred at the far end of a paddock. I couldn't see them well from this distance. One man was tall and muscular—no doubt one of the Graylord brothers. The other was a bit shorter and stockier but powerful looking—I recognized him from Dawn's descriptions as Theo Bosch, the barn manager.

I parked in the drive and quickly checked myself over in the rearview mirror. I patted down windswept strands of light brown hair, swept my cheeks with blush to make them look more angled than rounded, then swiped my full lips with a subtle gloss. Think conservative, I told myself, smoothing the collar of my silk blouse, which was the same shade of gray as my eyes.

I left my car and approached the house. Up close now, I could see that it needed tending. The stone could use a power wash, the peeling window frames and the worn-looking porch a fresh coat of paint. A slightly musty smell sent a shiver through me. I told myself it was just the presence of the river that was so close.

Before I reached the covered porch that winged around the river side of the building and held both a double swing and two Adirondack chairs, a woman of fifty-something opened the front door. Her thin, straight form was draped in a dreary, shapeless dress, and her unnaturally dark hair was slicked back from hawkish features.

"You'll be Chloe Morgan."

"I am indeed." I smiled, but it didn't echo in her lips, set in a straight, harsh line. "Shall I get my bags?"

"You're a bit ahead of yourself, wouldn't you say, miss? The master needs to approve you before you move in."

"I thought he already did that when he hired me."

"You'll wait in the parlor. He'll be with you anon."

Parlor? Anon? Was she kidding? She looked and sounded like something out of a Jane Austen novel.

"And you would be...?" I asked.

"Mrs. Avery to you," she said, her voice cool. "Watch that step. It needs to be replaced."

As did some missing spindles in the wood rail of the porch, I noticed as I stepped up carefully, wisps of fog rolling around my ankles as if trying to keep me from going inside.

I shook my head at my overactive imagination and hurried to catch up with her.

She showed me the room where I was to wait. I tried not to let my jaw drop. A parlor it was, and like something out of a museum. The marble fireplace, Oriental rug and furniture appeared to be nineteenth century—tables, sofa and chairs of walnut and a flowered upholstery that reflected the hand-stenciling on both the upper walls and ceiling. Still, the room had a shabby look to it. The wood could be refinished, the upholstery replaced.

I wondered that someone with so much money didn't keep the family estate in better shape.

"Miss Morgan?" came a deep voice from behind me. "You're punctual. Good."

I turned to meet the deep blue eyes of my employer, whom I had not yet met. His features were ruggedly attractive beneath thick black hair. A strand strayed across a high, broad forehead, and I was hard-pressed not to reach out and brush it back.

"My name is Chloe, Mr. Graylord."

"Damian will do."

Damian *would* do, I thought. He looked to be a dozen years my senior—of course, he would be, with a thirteen-year-old daughter—but he nearly took my breath away. Judging by his clothing and knee-high leather boots, he'd been riding. His six-foot frame was athletic. Buff…if thigh muscles accentuated by tight beige pants were any indication. A loose white cotton shirt whose neck was open and sleeves rolled up made him look at once elegant and rugged.

He arched a single dark eyebrow. "You're younger than I expected."

"I'm twenty-four, as stated in my résumé."

"But you look younger."

I wanted to argue with him that I was mature for my age and responsible, but I felt silence was called for. So instead I said, "Mr. Graylord, um, Damian…I thought you already hired me to be your daughter's summer tutor."

"Just a few questions before the agreement is finalized," he said, frowning as if at my naïveté. Then, his expression intense, he stepped closer. "Starting with…do you have a lover?"

Appalled, I took a step back. "Excuse me?"

"A boyfriend, then? Some male who might turn your head and distract you from your job?"

I blinked and took a sharp breath. For a moment I thought he was suggesting I would have duties other than seeing that Nissa was up to speed for the eighth grade in September. But then I decided he was being cautious, albeit overly, as to the reliability of the person who would tutor his daughter.

"No, I have no man in my life at the moment." Nor had I ever…at least, no one serious. Not that it was any of his business.

"I want to make certain you create a stable environment for Nissa."

I wanted to tell him that was *his* duty, but I doubted he would appreciate the observation, especially since I knew why he wanted reassurances. If it was to be believed, Dawn Reed, his daughter's homeschool teacher this past semester, up and eloped with some man no one knew about, not even me.

Only, I *didn't* believe it.

"I plan on doing my best," I said.

"You're committed to the full two months?"

"Committed. Absolutely."

"No distractions?"

"None," I lied.

He was the distraction. Damian Graylord and his brother Alex and perhaps every other person on Graylord Pastures. Someone here had the key to Dawn's disappearance, and I was determined to find it.

"Good. Then we have an acceptable working relationship."

He held out his hand, and I realized he wanted to shake on it. His hand engulfed mine, and the first thing I realized was that this was not the soft hand of a man who worked behind a desk but the hand of one used to physical labor. His skin was rough, his fingers lightly callused. The second thing I realized was that he held my hand a bit too long, and an electrifying sensation sizzled up my arm. And the way he was looking at me… heat flushed my cheeks. Wondering if this was some kind of test, I pulled my hand from his.

With the flick of a black eyebrow, he strode to the

fireplace and tugged on a fancy pull that flowed from the wall.

Just seconds later Mrs. Avery surfaced from somewhere. "You rang, sir?"

"Mrs. Avery, will you see that Nissa comes downstairs? I want her to meet her new tutor."

"Miss Nissa isn't upstairs, Mr. Damian. She's gone riding."

"I told her I wanted her here when Chloe arrived," he said tersely, making me uncomfortable.

"Yes, sir, and I reminded her."

"But she went, anyway?"

I could see Damian's cheek muscles working as he tried to control his aggravation. He lost the battle.

"How long ago was this?" he practically shouted.

"Twenty minutes or so."

"So she sneaked out when she saw her tutor arrive."

"I couldn't say."

"I'm going after her," he muttered. "When I get her back here, she'll be lucky if I don't skin her alive."

Startled by the threat of violence, I told myself Damian didn't actually mean that. Dawn had mentioned his temper, but she'd never said he'd used corporal punishment on his daughter.

Wishing I were anywhere but in this room, I asked meekly, "What would you like *me* to do?"

"Whatever you please!"

With that, Damian was out the door and I was off to a shaky start. The only one who seemed pleased was Mrs. Avery, who was wearing a satisfied smile.

"Perhaps you ought to get your bags now, miss. No

one will be made available to help you with them. You'll go through the back door into the kitchen. Take the rear stairs to the second floor. Your room is the one to the far left. The third floor is the attic, used for storage. You are not to go up there."

She left me, and I stood there, stunned for a moment, again wondering what I'd gotten myself into.

What was done was done, I told myself, as I exited the house to get my bags. I did not intend to leave until I had my answers. Hopefully not until I was reconnected with Dawn.

This past six-month period was the longest time we'd gone without seeing each other since meeting when I was fourteen, Dawn fifteen. When my mother died and my father abandoned me, Family Services placed me in a foster home with the Winstons. Removed from her alcoholic mother's custody, Dawn was already in residence. We bonded from the first day. She called me Ci-Ci, never Chloe—her version of Sissy, because she said we were just like sisters. We went to the same college, became roomies afterward, and we both took teaching jobs with the Chicago Public Schools.

Dawn would never just disappear on me if she could help it.

Outside, I looked toward the barn about a hundred yards away, where Damian mounted a dark bay and raced off across the grounds in the general direction of the river. As if we had some kind of connection I could not fathom, I felt his jumbled emotions.

I turned from him to gaze at the horses in the connected pastures—mares with their cavorting offspring. I'd always loved horses. Dawn and I both did. When we started teaching, we saved all our spare money to take riding lessons. I was no expert, but I wasn't bad. So, seeing the horses made me understand why Dawn had been drawn to this place. What I still didn't understand was why she left it without warning me.

Unlike my father, Dawn would never up and disappear on me if she could help it.

Once more I swore I would find her if it was the last thing I ever did.

DAMIAN CUT THROUGH the apple orchard, intent on getting to Nissa and bringing a quick end to her latest act of defiance. Her mother was gone for good, and the sooner she accepted that, the better.

Damn Priscilla! He guessed she'd loved Nissa in her own way, just loved money more.

Preoccupied as he was with solving the failing finances of the estate, he didn't need more problems from Nissa. She'd always been a wild child but a loving one. With Priscilla out of her life for good, her loving nature too often took a back seat to less admirable traits. In the last year, Nissa had made a concerted effort to actively illustrate her depression and anger, including ignoring her studies so that she'd been in danger of failing and falling a year behind in school.

Spotting her through the trees on Wild Cherry, a mare whose chestnut coat was nearly as red as Nissa's hair, Damian squeezed his legs, urging Sargent-Major to catch up. Leaning forward along the bay's neck, he whistled sharply the several-note call he used to bring in all his horses from pasture.

Cherry's ears went up, and the mare started prancing and trying to turn toward him. Nissa fought her, and though irritated with her rebelliousness, Damian also watched with pride as the thirteen-year-old took charge of her equally spirited mount.

The delay allowed him the time to catch up to his daughter just outside the orchard and in view of the river from high above. Another issue between them—he'd forbidden her to ride anywhere near the palisades if she was alone. He reached over and grabbed Cherry's halter.

"Enough," he said, slowing Sarge and bringing both horses to a halt. "You're in trouble now, young lady."

Nissa's eyes—a softer color than her mother's pure green—flashed her rebelliousness. "I was just exercising my mare."

"You could have done that early this morning. You waited purposely to insult your new tutor by not being there to meet her."

"I don't need a stupid tutor!"

Damian clenched his jaw so he wouldn't respond in kind. At the moment, her defiant expression reminded him of her mother, though she would never be as stunning as Priscilla. Someday Nissa would be striking, rather than beautiful, but right now she was in that awkward growing-up stage where none of her features seemed to work together in her best interests.

"I'll be the judge of what you need, young lady. And Chloe Morgan is *not* stupid. She will be a good summer companion for you." And a pleasant addition to the household. She was easy on the eyes and in personality. It would be a relief to have a woman of a subdued nature around for once. "When you return to your school in September, I want you to be able to keep up with your classmates."

"Who cares?" Nissa said sullenly.

"I care, Freckles, you know I do."

"Don't call me that! I'm not a little kid anymore."

"Then stop acting like one. Be the young lady I know you can be. Let's go back to the house so you can meet Chloe. And you'll apologize to her for your rudeness."

"Will not," Nissa muttered, jerking the reins and pulling the mare around so she was headed back to the house.

Following, Damian knew she would apologize, though it might kill her to do so. The ride back would give her time to consider her actions. She wasn't a terrible child, just one who was heartbroken at the loss of her mother. She didn't want to lose her father, too, so she would capitulate because she needed his approval.

The mild-mannered Miss Morgan might be exactly what Nissa needed to settle down. She'd given Dawn one hell of a time for a while, but Dawn hadn't taken any nonsense from Nissa, who had eventually come around and acted more like her old self. Not in the last month, though. Obviously, Nissa felt abandoned yet again.

Which brought him back to Miss Chloe Morgan. She came highly recommended by the agency who'd sent her. Damian only hoped she'd been sincere about meeting her obligations.

At least she wouldn't be a disruptive influence in the

household. Chloe was a pretty thing—heart-shaped face, dimpled right cheek, big gray eyes, trim body—not a real looker like Dawn, who'd been a blond bombshell and something of a tumultuous presence. By contrast, having Chloe Morgan around the estate would be peaceful and safe.

As they arrived back at the barn, Theo Bosch was there to meet them. The barn manager wasn't much older than Damian, but his dark blond hair was already thinning and he wore a billed cap to hide the fact.

Visually inspecting both horses as he always did when they came in from a ride, Theo muttered, "They need to be walked," as if they didn't always. "Clifford!" he yelled for the groom.

Not having the time to walk out the horses himself today, Damian dismounted and handed over the reins to the barn manager. "The new tutor has arrived."

"I'm aware of that."

There wasn't much that happened around the estate that Theo didn't notice—a fact that sometimes irritated Damian. "I don't know if Chloe rides or not, but I'll tell her a horse will be available for her use if she so desires."

"I'll pick one for her based on her experience," Theo said. An odd expression crossed his features. "So is this one more suitable than the last?"

Nissa gasped. Damian glanced back to see that she'd gone wide-eyed and her chin jutted out. She turned and fled toward the house.

Damian gave Theo an angry glare before he followed the girl to the house, where Nissa's voice carried to him through the open door.

"Chloe Morgan, where are you? Come down here and get this over with right now!"

Damian ran the last few yards to the house, and as he bounded up the steps, he heard the tutor answer.

"I'm right here, Nissa."

He entered the foyer as Chloe came down the stairs, the light from the windows glowing around her, making her appear ethereal and somewhat fragile.

"You're not to keep me waiting!"

"Nissa!" Damian growled.

But Chloe held out a hand, as if warning him to stay out of this. Shocked, Damian simply stared at her.

"You can count on me to be here for you for the whole summer, Nissa," Chloe said.

"No, I can't! I can't count on anyone! You're going to disappear like my mother did and then like Dawn did, so you might as well do it now!"

Before Chloe could respond, Damian lost the little temper he had left. "Keep it up, Nissa, and you won't need a tutor. I can still send you to the Grant School for Girls."

Damian was instantly sorry, of course, because Nissa's face crumpled, and tears flowed down her cheeks as she raced up the stairs past Chloe, who stood there staring at him accusingly.

Damian glared at her in return. She'd best know her place in this household, or she would be history.

Chapter Two

I wanted to follow and calm Nissa down, but I knew she needed a few minutes to get herself together first. Waiting until Nissa was out of earshot before turning back to Damian, I demanded, "Whatever were you thinking?"

I knew speaking to him this way wasn't the wisest of decisions, especially if I wanted to keep this job. His brow was furrowed and his mouth was a tight line. I could feel his anger washing over me, but I couldn't help myself. His threatening to send his daughter away—the idea of abandoning her when she needed him most—appalled me.

"I was thinking that I am the girl's father," he said stonily.

"Indeed you are. That gives you a great responsibility," I told him more coolly than I was feeling. My pulse jagged and suddenly I had trouble breathing. I choked out, "I hope you are up to it."

"*You* hope? You're merely my daughter's tutor—"

"And because of that, I have her best interests at heart." I felt myself winding up tight and my words coming out faster. "I don't just teach my students theory and then shut them out if the real world intrudes. Trust me, I know Nissa doesn't want to chase anyone away." I could identify with Nissa in a way he never could. "She's simply confused and trying to protect herself before someone else can leave her."

As I spoke, I saw Damian's features shift. A neutral expression replaced the anger.

Was this meant to relax me? I wondered.

Or did my heartfelt words actually affect him?

He gave me a curt nod and said, "Go see to your student, then."

I watched him leave the house before heading up the stairs. My knees felt like mush, but somehow I made it. Coming up against someone like Damian was intimidating. The kids I could handle—I didn't have a lot of experience dealing with difficult parents. Plus, Damian was so attractive that it unnerved me a little.

I pressed my ear to Nissa's door and heard her sobbing. My heart went out to the unhappy girl. I wanted to hold her in my arms and tell her everything would be okay…except I doubted she would let me and I didn't want to lie.

I knocked at her door, saying, "Nissa, this is Chloe. May I come in?"

"I guess."

I opened the door to find Nissa standing at the window, her narrow back stiff and turned to me. Her room was a typical one for a thirteen-year-old—little-kids' furniture but heartthrob posters on the yellow walls, a stuffed horse next to a laptop computer. The most prominent thing in the room, though, was the large tank of pretty fish set against the wall opposite the fireplace.

I said, "I thought we could use a few moments alone to get to know each other."

"Whatever."

"I am kind of new at this teaching thing, so I thought maybe you could help me."

She turned to give me a curious look, and from the smears of dirt across her cheeks—no doubt the dust from her ride—I could tell she'd wiped at the tears because she didn't want me to know she'd been crying. Her green eyes were muddied, stirred up by the emotional storm raging inside her.

"You want *me* to help *you?*" Nissa asked disbelievingly.

"Yes. To sort out what it is you need to work on over the summer."

"I am pretty bright, you know."

"I'm sure you are."

"I'm all caught up with my studies. My messing up was just a phase I was going through," she said as if she was all better now.

"Your father wants to make certain you stay caught up."

"Dad thinks I need a babysitter." She flounced herself across the bed, stomach down, and picked up a framed photo that she set on the bedside table.

"He doesn't consider you a baby, Nissa." I came a little closer, noticed the photograph was one of her and her mother, an exotic beauty with Nissa's hair and a brighter version of her eyes. "But perhaps he's too busy taking care of the horses to give you the company he thinks you need."

"He *does* think I'm a baby. He won't even tell me the truth about Mama."

"Divorces are difficult—"

"Divorce? Yeah, I imagine he'd tell you that. My mother is dead."

I frowned. "Dead?"

"She just wasn't here one day. She was gone. And I saw Dad take her things out of the house." All gawky arms and legs, she scrambled to sit on the edge of the mattress. "He said Mama didn't want to live here anymore and that she would be happier elsewhere. But if that was true, *I* wouldn't be here, because Mama would never leave me. She would have taken me with her."

I didn't know what to think. Dawn hadn't told me anything about Nissa believing her mother was dead. "Perhaps your mother *couldn't* take you with her."

"Then why doesn't she come to see me? Or call me? Other kids in my class have divorced parents. Usually they live with their mothers."

"You don't want to be with your father?" I asked, wondering if she had good reason.

"Of course I want to be with him. When he's not angry at me, Dad is the best. If Mama was still alive, I would be living with her and seeing Dad on the weekends."

"It often works that way, but not always."

When my mother died, my father left me to the system and never looked back. Not exactly the same situation, but close enough. I understood what she was feeling. The sense of loss and abandonment subsided but never fully went away. At times, I still felt all alone—unlovable, even.

Poor kid. Nissa couldn't believe that her mother didn't want her and so she had to pretend she was dead. She looked ready to cry again. I couldn't stop myself from crossing to her and smoothing the hair from her face. She blinked rapidly, as if she was trying to stop the tears from coming.

"It's all right," I said. "I understand."

I didn't cling to the moment. Nissa didn't know me well enough to throw herself into my arms. She didn't know me at all. But now I had a lot of insight into her.

"How about you show me what you and Dawn worked on this spring?"

We spent the next quarter of an hour going over Nissa's books and a binder of work. Dawn had done a good job homeschooling her. Nissa was definitely ready to go back to school and keep up with her classmates. But she still needed to deal with her emotions.

"Very good," I said, "though I think you could use an extra boost in the composition department."

"Composition?"

"Writing skills. I want you to start keeping a journal."

"You mean like a diary."

"Sort of. You can write about your thoughts. Or about a great ride you have on your horse. Or about the beauty of the river. Your choice. Every afternoon, I'd like you to take a little time and write."

"Who's going to read it?"

"Just me, if that's what you want."

"That's what I want."

"All right, then. We'll start tomorrow after breakfast. I see you have a computer. Are you online?"

"Yeah. I got Dad to go wireless, so I don't have to go to his study. It's set up so I can work on my laptop anywhere in the house. Outside, too. Why?"

"Because you're going to use the Internet to help you study."

The promise sparked a seed of interest. Good. I explained how I would pick one subject per morning and she would get to search the Internet to expand her knowledge on a specific topic. To my relief, Nissa seemed pleased, if not outright enthusiastic.

We'd made a start.

On my way out, I paused at the tank to watch the colorful fish dart from one side to the other, through greenery and around the decorations that created an underwater fantasyland. A bright blue fish hid in a hollow castle tower, while a striped one disrupted the shiny stones at the bottom of the tank, making me wonder what he was hoping to find.

"Great fish tank," I said. "Do you take care of it yourself?"

"Ever since I was a kid." Nissa sounded as if she were old and worldly now. "Dad said if I wanted pets of any kind, I would have to take care of them. I don't let anyone else touch the fish or the tank. I do everything myself."

"It's really beautiful."

Nissa glowed at my compliment, and I silently congratulated Damian for giving his daughter a sense of responsibility at such a young age.

I returned to my room, narrow but with a view of the woods and a glimpse of the bluffs and river beyond. This was definitely a servant's room—twin bed, single chest of drawers topped with two fat candles, smallish oval mirror, rag rug on wooden floors, simple fireplace without embellishment. Everything was white or some shade of blue, cool and calming, if a little tattered.

This had been Dawn's room. I wondered that she hadn't complained to me. Dawn liked space and brilliant colors and luxuries. Perhaps she'd been content with the view from two directions, this being a corner room. Or perhaps it had been the male company—Damian and his younger brother, Alex—that had made her content here. Dawn had always needed men around her, had needed their attention to make her feel worthy.

A noise overhead like a scrape of nails on board sent an uncomfortable sensation down my spine. Well, I had been warned the attic was off-limits to me, so whoever was up there was none of my business.

I glanced at my laptop sitting on my bed and decided to check my e-mail since the house was set up for wireless. Of course, what I looked for as I did each day was an e-mail from Dawn—we'd been in contact at least once a week until she'd disappeared.

Nothing.

The note she'd left, saying she was eloping, had been enough to keep the authorities from starting a missing persons search. That, plus the fact that there had been no suspicion of foul play. An adult was allowed to be missing if she so pleased, and the authorities wouldn't get involved.

At least, that's what the head of the agency who'd sent us both here had told me. I'd waited and waited to hear from Dawn, telling me she was happily married. I never did. But it just wasn't like Dawn not to check in with me, her best friend. Especially if she'd gotten married! I applied for the tutor position myself via the same employment agency she'd used. Rather than deal with the situation via long-distance telephone, I'd decided to come and do so in person, from the inside. I wanted to see that elopement note myself, to see if the signature was really Dawn's. I wondered if the note still existed.

Somehow, I had to find out what happened to my friend. Something was wrong with that story—I knew it. I could feel it in my bones—Dawn was in trouble.

Booming male voices jarred me out of my thoughts. Two men were having a heated discussion outside, practically below my window. I recognized one of the voices as Damian's, but I didn't have a clue as to who the other man was. I moved to the window to see.

"I told you more than once, Relentless is not for sale," Damian said.

"C'mon, man, everyone knows you're in trouble here after losing Centaur. You can recoup some of your losses."

"Not if I don't have stallions to bring in the stud fees that keep this place running."

The man with Damian was of equal height and build, but his hair was lighter. He seemed to be good-looking in an ordinary way.

"You can't afford to be so dismissive, Graylord."

"Listen, Larson, tell your old man he's not going to get hold of my farm or my stock."

"You should have sold us Centaur when we made you an offer. Don't make that mistake again."

"Is that a threat?"

"I meant it as good advice, but take it as you will!"

With that, the stranger spun on his heel and stalked away.

Even from this distance, I could see the tension gripping Damian. He looked as if he wanted to punch someone or something, but in the end, he, too, stalked off.

Watching Damian head for the barns, I had trouble taking my eyes off his imposing figure. Why would he be so angry that someone had made an offer to buy one of the stallions? Or perhaps he wasn't angry with the man but with his own situation. Apparently he'd lost a stallion….

I shook my head. The farm's troubles and finances were not my concern. Nissa was.

My mind wandered to what Nissa had told me about her mother's disappearance.

I came to Graylord Pastures to solve one mystery, and now it seemed I had two. Priscilla Graylord. Dawn had said nothing about the woman being dead.

Now curious to find out more about Nissa's mother, I wandered down the back stairs into the kitchen where Merle Pope was humming to herself as she cooked. Merle was a short, round woman with a pleasant way about her. She was the only one who'd smiled at me since I arrived.

I sniffed the air. "Something smells wonderful."

"Dinner. Pork roast with roasted potatoes and asparagus. Haven't started the asparagus yet. It only needs to cook for five minutes. Most people overcook it, you know, so that you can't hold out a stalk but what it droops. It's best lightly cooked so there's a bit of crunch left to the stalk. Then it has a slight nutty flavor."

"I'm sure it will be delicious. Oh, I'm making assumptions here." For all I knew, I could be relegated to the kitchen and a different menu altogether.

"Don't worry, you'll be eating with the family," Merle said. "The table needs a woman, what with the harridan gone."

"You're not talking about the last teacher?"

"Dawn? No, she was all right once you got to know her. I was referring to Mr. Damian's ex-wife."

"She's not dead, then?"

"Whatever gave you that idea? Ah, Miss Nissa. Poor child." Merle clucked to herself.

"It is a shame that her mother never sees her."

"It's a blessing, if you want my opinion."

"Your opinion is not called for in family matters," said Mrs. Avery, having entered the kitchen unannounced. "You should be concentrating on dinner." Then she looked at me. "And you, miss, should keep your nose where it belongs."

Merle simply rolled her eyes at me.

Dinnertime couldn't come fast enough. The dining room was formal, the furnishings probably original to the house. I admired the intricately carved legs of the table and buffet. The wood was beautiful, but once again I thought the room had gone too long without proper attention. The formal draperies were frayed and needed replacing, the walls needed a fresh coat of paint, and the fireplace mantel could use a bit of restoration.

Alone in the room, I stared out the windows. The fog was rising, and a rumble in the distance told me rain was coming.

A few minutes later I found myself seated across from Nissa. Damian took the head of the table, while the place across from him remained conspicuously unoccupied.

"We won't be waiting for Alex," Damian told Mrs. Avery. "If he can't get himself to the table on time, he can eat whatever is leftover."

"Yes, Mr. Damian."

"Never fear, your brother is here," came a voice from the next room.

I turned to see a younger, more conventionally handsome version of the older Graylord brother enter the dining room and approach the table. His hair was lighter, medium golden brown, and his eyes were a less intense shade of blue. He went past his waiting chair and straight to Nissa. He kissed her on the cheek.

"How's my favorite niece?"

"You mean your *only* niece."

Though she protested, Nissa was enthralled by her uncle, if the color in her cheeks was any indication.

Alex swept around the table toward me. "And you must be the new tutor, Chloe Morgan." He took my hand and kissed it. "Enchanted."

"Lord, Alex, do sit down and behave yourself."

Alex ignored his brother and held my gaze. "Am I behaving quite terribly?"

"I find you quite charming, Mr.—"

"Alex. Without the mister, thank you. We're very informal here."

"I hadn't noticed."

"Well, *I'm* informal."

"Alex!"

Alex gave Damian an amused look. "All right, devil-boy, I'm sitting."

Devil-boy? Damian? I glanced at him from under my lashes, but Damian was snapping his cloth napkin open and calling over Mrs. Avery to serve. She carried plates of food from the buffet and set them on the chargers before each one of us.

"You wouldn't think it to look at him now," Alex told me in a loud whisper, "but my brother was once quite a hooligan. That's what Mother used to call him."

"Enough reminiscing," Damian growled, his eyes practically shooting sparks at his brother, "or your food *will* get cold."

Alex laughed and Nissa put her napkin to her mouth to cover her smirk. I bit the inside of my cheek so I wouldn't react at all. I found it hard to believe Damian was ever a fun-loving boy.

As we ate, Damian didn't say much, almost as if he was lost in his own head. Every once in a while he gave me a piercing look. I felt his eyes on me as clearly as a touch.

"I heard you had a visit from Jack Larson this afternoon," Alex said suddenly.

Damian grunted. "Made me another offer for Relentless."

"Big surprise. I assume you told him no?"

"Of course I did."

"Are you sure you shouldn't at least consider the offer?"

Damian's expression darkened. "That would be the

start of the end." But then he seemed to catch himself and gave his daughter a quick look. "Everything is going to work out all right. No need to worry."

Alex, too, gave Nissa a quick look. "Yeah, you're right. Let's talk about something more pleasant…."

Alex turned the conversation on a dime. I found his presence welcome. For the rest of the meal, he kept the mood at the table light and Nissa giggling.

I warmed to him and imagined Dawn being drawn to his personality, as well.

For weeks before she'd disappeared, Dawn had teased me via her daily e-mails about a possible romance in the making. This might have worked in with the elopement story if she hadn't claimed both Graylord brothers were courting her. She'd never mentioned any other man. The whole time she wrote me, I suspected Dawn's vivid imagination had been at work again. From the time we were teenagers, I realized Dawn was so desperate for love that she thought any man who was kind to her had deeper feelings.

Both of the Graylord men were attractive and compelling—Damian with power, Alex with charm.

Damian with Dawn? I couldn't see it. I'd only met him this morning and already I figured Dawn with her outgoing ways probably exasperated him. But Alex was much cooler and fun loving. He'd probably liked Dawn.

A sudden thought had me gulping a great swallow of water so that I could get my food down. What if Dawn had a thing with Alex and Damian had disapproved? How far would Damian go to see that his brother didn't hook up with the wrong sort of woman—one who came from no money or social standing?

Would he make her disappear?

Like his wife?

"I NEED TO WORK OFF some energy after that wonderful meal," I said to Nissa as we pushed away from the table after consuming big slices of homemade berry pie. "A walk is in order. Would you like to join me?"

She smiled. "Sure—"

"Not tonight," Damian said.

"Dad!"

"It's going to rain—"

"I won't melt."

"—and you know I don't want you off the grounds after dark."

Damian flashed me a look I interpreted as a warning. As if I would know his rules without his telling me.

"We'll walk tomorrow, then. In full daylight. Assuming the sun is out." I couldn't help my sarcasm, but if Damian noticed, he didn't respond.

"Dad, you've got to stop treating me like a baby!"

"You'll always be my baby."

"Eeeouw!"

Nissa raced up the stairs, her father following at a more leisurely pace as I headed for the front door.

"Walking at night alone isn't wise."

I turned to find Damian stopped halfway up the stairs. "Are you saying being outside in this area isn't safe?"

"You don't know the territory. If you're set on it, take one of the flashlights by the door." He pointed to a rack that also held umbrellas. "Accidents happen in the dark. And in the rain."

I ignored the shiver that slid through me. "Normally I run. If I don't get some fresh air and exercise, I'll have trouble getting to sleep."

"There are other things you can do to sleep."

Before I could ask him to clarify, he was gone. Alex was still there, leaning against the dining room doorjamb. He grinned at me and his expression was appreciative.

"You're not quite the lamb you seem."

"We all have our strengths."

"Mmm, quiet strength…perhaps the most effective suit of all," Alex said, narrowing his gaze on me. "I would take that walk with you, but unfortunately I have prior plans."

Feeling a bit itchy under his intense gaze, I said, "I'll be fine."

"As long as you don't get caught in the storm. Until tomorrow, then…."

We both stepped outside. He went to the Jaguar sitting in the drive, and I grabbed a flashlight before heading into the damp evening without a raincoat or umbrella. I liked the rain and getting wet didn't scare me. Besides, I'd driven all day and needed to stretch my legs. I headed away from the pastures and gazebo and toward the stand of trees between the house and river bluffs. The night was warm and soft with mist. I was drawn to water—kind of natural since I lived so close to Lake Michigan. I ran along the lake or rode on the bike path nearly every day, weather permitting.

I sensed the river ahead and I was drawn to it.

Thunder rumbled closer now and lightning sent shards of white through the sky, but I was oblivious to the threat of the imminent storm. The walk to the bluffs was short. Once I was in the open, away from the trees, the wind buffeted me, and the rush of the river's current was like a song in my blood. I stood there, quiet, my eyes closed for a moment, and expanded my mind. A type of meditation had seen me through a lot of bad times, and I used it now to keep me on an even keel.

I think of Dawn…my friend…my foster sister… I see her beautiful face…smiling…eyes sparkling…that mischievous look she gets when she's going to do something she knows she shouldn't.

"Dawn," I call to her, "where are you? Why have you abandoned me? Has something happened to you?"

The smile on her face melts…her eyes widen and the look in them is unsettling, as if she's afraid…or perhaps horrified.

"What happened to you?" I ask, feeling choked by the emotions that suddenly surge through me as I face what I fear the most. "Tell me. Give me some sign."

But her image begins to waver…my pulse pounds as I try to keep Dawn's face sharp in my mind… I am defeated when she melts into the ether….

I opened my eyes. I was crying and the evening mist was turning to drizzle and slicking my face. The change in temperature was forcing clouds of fog from the river up over the bluffs to drift along the earth and then rise in anemic plumes. For a moment I felt lost in a nightmare land where I was alone and vulnerable.

As I headed back toward the house, a soft sound echoed across the bluffs—the blowing sound a horse made through its nose when running. But surely no horse was out there, not at night. Not alone. Damian Graylord wouldn't risk his prize stock.

Still, I heard the even thud of shod feet on earth and more horselike breathing. I moved toward the sounds, which seemed to be coming through some trees, and moved the flashlight beam around. Nothing. I whistled low. If a horse had gotten loose from its pasture, I meant to take it back. I whistled again as the rain started hitting the treetops harder. It was relatively dry in the fog-fingered woods. I got a glimpse of pale hide through the trees and whistled again.

Suddenly I saw it—a gray horse wheeled around through the mists and, looking like something out of a dream, headed for me too fast. It didn't slow, and I was directly in its path. I jumped out of the way and bounced against a tree trunk and lost my flashlight just before the horse nearly ran me over.

Heart thundering, I gathered myself together, but when I looked down the path, the horse was gone and all I saw in the electrical zap of lightning was the stillness of an eerie, translucent landscape.

It was as if the horse had faded into the mists.

Chapter Three

A crack of thunder loud enough to shake the trees made me quake inside. The following series of lightning strikes sent shafts of light like narrow swords through the woods around me, and I realized my foolishness. Lightning was drawn to tall objects, trees in particular. Most forest fires were started by an electrical storm.

I couldn't find the dropped flashlight, so I started for the house but danced in a circle to see if I could catch another glimpse of the horse among the trees. I didn't.

I left the woods and started across an open space, the ground beneath my feet quickly turning into muck from the downpour. I rushed as if I was afraid of getting wet, when in reality, it was my fear of what happened to Dawn that was chasing me. I didn't want to think about it. I wanted to believe I would find her whole and well and happily married—holed up somewhere, oblivious of anything but love—and that I would have reason to scold her for giving me the scare of my life.

Only I didn't believe it.

So I ran with my head down, trying not to think, trying not to let my mind follow the darker path. I forced myself faster, narrowing my focus on the ground in front of me where I would step next.

I didn't see the feet until I ran into the man. I plunged into him full force and he stepped back with the impact and threw a steadying arm around me.

"Easy, there."

I looked up at the man and nearly screamed, "Damian!"

"Are you all right?"

"Of course," I said, trying not to let him hear the fear in my voice. "I was just getting out of the storm."

"You should have taken an umbrella."

As he had. I was dripping but no longer being pelted with rain. Instead I was pressed against his broad chest under his umbrella. I was too aware of this man of whom I need be suspicious. I couldn't trust anyone until I knew the truth. No one but Nissa.

I slipped my hand between us to push him away and could feel his strong heartbeat under my palm. My breath caught in my throat and my pulse fluttered.

"Let's get you back to the house where you can get warm and dry," he said.

I didn't tell him I was warm enough already because of him. He turned me toward the house but kept his hand on my waist, my hip pressed against his. Nothing personal on his part, I was sure, but it felt uncomfortably personal on mine.

We're maybe a hundred yards from the house. I waited until we ran up under the porch before I said, "You'd better check on your horses."

"Already done."

"Then you know one is loose."

"No. All present and accounted for."

"But there's a horse out there." I glanced back the way we had come.

"Where? In the woods?"

"Yes. I was coming back from the bluffs when I thought I heard it."

"It was probably the storm. The wind out here is tricky."

"I tell you, he was there, a gray Thoroughbred."

Damian laughed at me. "You have quite an imagination. The only pale horse on the estate was a valuable gray stud that died in a terrible fall off the bluffs last month."

Goose bumps prickled up my spine. He must mean Centaur, the stallion Jack Larson had mentioned. "There are no other grays on the farm?"

"Not a one."

"What about a neighbor's horse?"

"There are a couple of bays in the area. Chestnuts. An Appaloosa. No grays." He smothered another laugh. "You must have seen a ghost horse."

Bristling at Damian's mocking tone, I bit down a tart retort.

He placed a hand on the small of my back, saying, "Come on, let's go inside."

We headed for the porch, with me too aware of the imprint of each of his fingers. I wanted to run ahead, but I didn't want him to know he affected me.

The moment we got into the foyer, Damian said, "Change and then come downstairs. The dryer is in the mudroom by the back door. And you can warm up by the fire."

The last thing in the world I wanted right now was to spend any extended amount of time in his company—I would rather take a hot shower and read before going to bed than chance more unwanted attraction—but I could hardly refuse. So I determined to use the opportunity to get what information about Dawn's disappearance that I could from him.

"All right. A fire sounds good."

I was soaked through, and the June night air was chilly. I ran up to my room and shed the wet clothes. Out the window, the rain was driving down hard like an opaque curtain. As I dried myself with a towel from the washstand, I remembered Damian's arm around me, I felt again his fingers at the small of my back, and my nipples tightened in response.

I wondered what it would be like to have his hand in other, more intimate places.

And then I shook the fantasy. It wouldn't be smart to develop a thing for my employer. I didn't know him. I didn't know that he didn't play a part in Dawn's disappearance.

I dried my hair and combed it out, then pulled on terry pants and a long-sleeved top. Gathering the wet clothes, I descended the back stairs and stopped to put them in the dryer before heading for the study.

The room smelled like a combination of old leather and furniture wax and smoke from the fire. Floor-to-ceiling shelves filled with books lined two of the walls, and an old-fashioned desk with a new-fashioned computer sat between a pair of mullioned windows. It was the kind of room that set off the imagination…a room meant for clandestine meetings where plots were hatched and crimes planned.

Damian was ensconced in a club chair in front of the fire, a glass of amber liquid in his hand. He appeared every bit the master of the house. His brow was furrowed as he stared into the flames. I wondered what troubled him—my story about the gray horse or something darker?

He turned his gaze to me. "So soon. Both punctual and a quick change."

"Personally, I find that men take far longer at grooming than women do."

His eyebrows flicked upward but he didn't respond to my smart response. I didn't know if it was true and I hadn't been with enough men myself to generalize. My one intimate relationship lasted more than a year, but in the end hadn't worked out. James said it was me, that I couldn't open up enough to let real love in, and that he wanted more than the physical passion I provided.

Perhaps he'd been correct. My father's abandoning me at a critical age made me cautious with men. So cautious that I balked at trying it again.

"Can I offer you a drink? Brandy? Wine?"

"A glass of red would be nice."

I warmed myself by the fire and Damian went to a liquor cabinet built into the shelving. He poured red wine for me and topped up his brandy. He handed me my glass and clinked his to it.

"To a successful match. That is, you and Nissa," he hurried to add as if I might misunderstand.

My turn to raise an eyebrow at him. And to take advantage of the opening.

I sipped at the wine, a fine dry vintage, and said, "Nissa and Dawn got along, didn't they?"

"Nissa had great affection for Dawn," he said without sounding as if he shared that feeling. "It made it all the harder on the girl when Dawn left without saying goodbye."

"Yes, the agency mentioned something about a note—"

"Saying she was eloping," Damian finished for me. "Not that the agency should have mentioned anything of my business. The note was very cut-and-dried."

"Was that like her?"

"I didn't think so, but I've been fooled by women before."

I assumed he was referring to his ex-wife, Priscilla, and wondered if his serious expression when I entered the room was for her. I sipped at the wine and shifted in my chair so I could see his reactions to my questions more directly.

"Maybe if the note wasn't like Dawn...well, what if there was no truth to the elopement story?"

"And she just took off and lied about why? That wouldn't make sense."

True, but I wanted to explore all possibilities. "Perhaps something else was going on that you didn't know about and Dawn didn't leave on her own."

Damian flicked an eyebrow upward. "You do have an overactive imagination. First you think you see a ghost horse, now you think the last teacher met foul play? Who would have written the note, then?"

I clenched my jaw at his repeated sarcasm about the

ghost horse and told myself to remain cool. "I'm just playing 'what if' here. Was the note in her handwriting?"

"It was written on the computer, actually," he said, indicating the desk opposite the fireplace.

"A signature?"

He shook his head and a furrow creased his brow. "Just her name typed."

"Then how do you know something didn't happen to her?"

"Look, she packed her things and stole out in the middle of the night. The authorities were satisfied no foul play was involved. Why aren't you?"

I felt his increase in emotions like a physical force. I tried to read him. He was angry, but I think not at me. I decided to keep my tone light.

"You sound irritated."

"It's just that I've been over this and over this."

I wondered if the authorities were as casual about Dawn's disappearance as he made it sound. Or was it Damian himself who questioned what really happened to my friend? I didn't want to think he was annoyed because he had something to do with her disappearance.

"Why the twenty questions?" he asked. "You didn't even know the woman. Did you?"

My stomach knotted at the reminder of my charade. Damian had no way of connecting us—I had done my querying through the employment counselor who actually was a friend of Dawn's and mine. I avoided his question.

"I think it's important that I have as much knowledge as possible about the situation in this household so I can understand Nissa better. She seems emotionally fragile, and I need information if I am to help her."

"I'm here to see to her emotional needs!" he said brusquely. "You see to her studies."

Not the response I hoped for. I realized my interview was at an end. Damian was obviously getting exasperated and wasn't going to be more forthcoming. At least not tonight. So I took one last sip of my wine and rose.

"Thank you for the drink and the fire. I'm quite warmed up now, and I think it's time I call it an evening. I've had a very long day."

"Pleasant dreams, then."

More sarcasm? Or did Damian mean this? I couldn't tell. He was once again preoccupied with his own thoughts.

Tension followed when I left the study. I fetched my clothes from the dryer. They were still a bit damp but they would dry on hangers. I took the back stairs to my room, where finally I relaxed and changed into my favorite nightgown—a calf-length white cotton shift edged with lace.

Exhausted yet not sleepy, I stood at the window and watched and listened to the drumming rain and the nervous nickering of horses in their barns. The windows had overhangs and were fairly dry, so I opened one and let the fresh smells and soothing sounds fill my room. The storm had lightened a bit and I stared out to the woods and to the small area of the bluffs beyond.

My ghost horse did not do a command performance for me.

My bed awaited, narrow but comfortable.

As my eyes fluttered closed, I pictured Dawn in my mind's eye. She was beautiful and happy and laughing.

And I knew it was a lie.

Dawn...my friend...the sister of my heart...what really happened to you?

The patter of rain lulled me to sleep.

DAMIAN WAS DOZING before the fire when a loud clunk brought him awake. "Who's there?"

"Just me, devil-boy." Alex strolled into the study and poured himself a drink.

"That nickname is getting old."

"Just like it's owner."

Damian roused himself and pulled a hand through his hair. How long had he been sleeping? He checked his watch and was surprised to see it was barely ten-thirty.

"What are you doing home so early, Alex? I thought you had a date."

"Bored. I don't think I'll be seeing her again."

"How many women do you go through in a year?"

"Jealous?"

After the mess with Priscilla, Damian wasn't in a hurry to repeat his mistake by being attracted to the wrong sort of woman. Too bad Dawn hadn't been more intuitive in that regard.

"I have too many other things on my mind."

"Then you need a distraction...like the pretty new schoolteacher."

Irritation sizzled through him. "Stay away from this one, Alex."

"Ah, so you're interested in her for yourself?"

Damian didn't answer. Something in him responded to Chloe Morgan. She was soft in nature, yet she seemed capable of holding her own. He sensed there was more going on with her than she let on. It wouldn't do to think along those lines, of course. She was Nissa's summer tutor and that was it as far as he was concerned.

But he didn't want Alex messing with her, either, not like he had with Dawn.

Alex plopped into the chair next to him, saying, "If you don't make a move on the comely Miss Morgan, you won't mind if I do, right?"

Knowing Alex was messing with him now, Damian wearily asked, "Will you ever act your age and settle down?"

"When the right woman comes along."

Thinking of the string of women Alex had gone through over the past several years, Damian asked, "Who would that be?"

"One with enough money to afford the lifestyle to which I would like to become accustomed away from here."

Damian had heard it all before. "What's wrong with this life?"

Alex thought he wanted a different one...only, he didn't know what. Damian figured it went back to their boyhood rivalry, when Alex continually attempted to one-up him.

"Take a realistic look around you, Damian. This place needs a ton of money to make it shine again. It's sliding down the tubes."

"We're not going to lose Graylord Pastures!"

"No, we'll probably get by somehow while the walls crumble around us."

"Then, figure out a way to get us the business we need to pull out of the hole."

"My specialty is promotions, not miracles." Alex splashed back his brandy. "Now, if we could ever find Great-great-great-grandmother Anna's diamonds…"

"Don't put stock in fairy tales," Damian said. "I'm sure the Equine Diamonds were sold a century ago to keep this place going. If they ever existed in the first place."

The tale of the Equine Diamonds had lured generations of Graylords to find them, but no one ever had.

"Then we need a miracle, devil-boy."

"We need a miracle."

I WANDER ALONG the bluffs, my feet stirring white clouds of fog that rise around me and encompass my body like snakes. The air is thick and I can hardly breathe, yet I go on…searching…trying to find her.

Hoofbeats drum across the ground, the sound muffled. I turn and turn and turn…looking…searching….

A shape pushes at the fog and forms an equine head. It comes at me in slow motion. The head, mane floating along a breeze…then the body, tail raised…finally the rider, hair whipping around her face….

"Dawn!" I cry, elated. I have found her at last.

But the horse and rider run straight through me, ghosts both….

I awoke in a sweat. Hot and cold. Feverish and washed over by the wind wailing through the open window. The storm had renewed itself, and the transparent curtains flew toward me like ghosts accompanied by a spray of mist. Thunder shook me in my bed and lightning electrified the sky so brightly, it illuminated my room.

I swore I saw something in the shadows.

My chest squeezed, and I gasped, "Who's there?"

No answer. Maybe I imagined it, part of the nightmare.

More lightning, and I caught movement this time. I thought fast. A weapon…what could I use?

And then the figure drew closer and I saw that it was Nissa.

"Nissa, is something wrong? Are you afraid of storms?"

She whispered one word. "Mama…"

Her eyes were open and she was moving but she was asleep. They say not to wake a sleepwalker. So, gently I turned her to the door and walked with her back to her room.

The door was open. Inside, the room was lit only by the fish tank that glowed softly against the wall. I got her into the bed and tucked the covers around her, then smoothed the tangled red hair from her forehead.

"Love you, Mama," she said with a sigh. And then her breathing said she was asleep.

Wondering how often she walked in her sleep and whether or not Damian knew about it, I left the room thinking I would have to talk to him about it.

I was almost back inside my own room when I heard a noise overhead. I looked up as if I could see through the ceiling. I heard it again. A bang. I was not imagining this. Not a part of my dream. Perhaps the storm forced open a window that needed closing.

Another bang as I entered my room—one that gave me a start.

I would never sleep if the noise overhead continued. And it was too late to wake anyone. I would have to fix whatever was wrong myself. I flipped the switch but the room lights didn't go on. The storm must have knocked out the power.

I found candles on my dresser and now knowing why they were there, lit them. Then I took one and left the room again to head for the back stairs. I didn't get but one foot on the first step before another door opened and I turned to see Mrs. Avery, her pale face ghostly in the candlelight. Her pencil-thin eyebrows winged up in question.

"And where do you think you're going, miss?"

Chapter Four

"Mrs. Avery," I said, trying to sound natural over the pounding of my heart. "I heard a noise overhead."

"Your imagination."

"No, really. I heard something earlier, as well."

"The house is ancient but settles still."

"It wasn't a creak or a groan, but more like a bang. I thought maybe a shutter had gotten loose. I thought I would just go check."

"That's your problem, miss. You think too much. It's not for you to decide anything about this household. And I told you myself that the attic is off-limits to you."

I flushed with a combination of embarrassment and irritation. "I'm sorry… I couldn't sleep for the noise." I couldn't help but feel defensive.

"All right, then," Mrs. Avery said, her tone exasperated. "I shall check on the attic myself and fix whatever it is that disturbs you. Though, if it isn't the wind, it's undoubtedly squirrels."

I didn't have any arguments left, so I nodded and descended the few stairs I'd taken. "Thank you," I mumbled as I headed for my room. I glanced back only once to satisfy myself that Mrs. Avery was, indeed, climbing to the attic.

The woman disliked me. Why? Did she feel I was usurping her somehow? Had she felt the same way about Dawn?

Shivering at the thought, I opened my bedroom door. Once inside my room, I blew out the candles. I climbed into bed and stared at the ceiling overhead as noises seemed to skitter from one direction and then the other. The sounds quickly subsided, and I heard a creak from the hallway—the stairs, no doubt, as Mrs. Avery descended. If she'd found squirrels in the attic, no doubt she'd chased them away for good.

Then I was listening only to the wind battering at the exterior of the old house. I let it fill my mind like white noise and concentrated on it to relax, until at last I drifted off….

THE NEXT MORNING the electricity was back on and the sun was shining brightly. As a matter of fact, the weather was perfect. The sun had chased away the clouds, the winds had died down to an errant breeze, and the air was warm and thick with the scent of trees and grass well-pleased by the rain.

"Let's work outside after breakfast," I suggested to my charge. "I'm assuming we can connect to the Internet from the gazebo."

Nissa shrugged. "Maybe." But she didn't sound in the least enthusiastic.

Still, I thought the gazebo would do well for my purposes. "Let's try."

So after breakfast, which we ate alone—the Graylord brothers apparently were early risers so they could see to the needs of the horses—we packed up our laptops and took them to the gazebo.

The large, weathered cedar structure with a shingled roof decorated with a weathervane was tired looking but nevertheless inviting. Boxes of brilliant flowers skimmed the rails in the openings, and in addition to a large padded "window seat" on one side, it was furnished with a round glass table and padded wicker chairs.

"Is something wrong?" I asked Nissa when she stood on the steps, seeming reluctant to follow me inside. "Don't you like the gazebo?"

"I used to come out here with my mother for afternoon tea."

"If coming here upsets you, you should have told me. We can go sit on the front porch."

"No. It's okay."

Wearing an expression of mulish determination, Nissa ran up the steps, set her laptop down on the table and threw herself into a chair. Her fingers dug into the wicker arms, and her attention was focused elsewhere. I turned and followed her gaze. Damian and two men I had not yet met—one leading a big bay—were deep in conversation.

"I take it you like horses."

"I *love* horses!" Nissa's expression transformed her plain face into one more appealing. "I'm going to be a trainer."

"What kind of trainer?"

She rolled her eyes. "Someone who trains horses, of course."

"But what kind of horses?" I pressed, having read everything I could about them once I'd decided to take lessons. "Or perhaps I should ask—train horses to do what? Thoroughbreds to race or become hunter-jumpers? Or are you interested in dressage?"

Nissa blinked at me and shrugged. Obviously, she hadn't thought the training thing through.

"Why don't we make training the focus of this morning's lesson, then." I'd already figured going with some topic about horses would appeal to her.

"You mean I should figure out what kind of trainer I want to be?"

"Well, you don't have to decide that now. But perhaps you could find information on different kinds of trainers so you can see your options."

The assignment proved to be a stroke of genius. Enthusiasm for the subject won over Nissa's hesitation at working in the gazebo. It even won over her distrust of me.

I did a little Internet research of my own so that I would have enough information on trainers to ask her pertinent questions about her research. After which, noting that Nissa was still humming away, I checked my e-mail.

No message from Dawn.

I sent my friend another plea to contact me, but this time it bounced back to me with a message that her e-mail box was full. A sense of doom I didn't want to acknowledge pushed me back into my chair.

I don't know how long I sat there, mind empty of

even one positive thought, before I realized Nissa was staring at me.

I flushed guiltily and gathered my thoughts. "So, what have you found so far? Anything interesting?"

"Are you okay?"

Now I felt doubly guilty. Nissa didn't need more worry. "Hey, I'm fine. I was just letting my mind wander, I guess."

"Yeah, I do that sometimes. My teacher at my school said it's why I was failing."

Though I wanted to ask if the teacher was correct, I held back the question. If Nissa broached the topic of her mother, I would gladly lend an ear and some reassuring words, but I didn't want to spoil the morning when we'd just gotten started.

So I forced myself to concentrate on her litany of jobs having to do with horse training, which covered everything from Thoroughbred racehorses to quarter horses used to round up cows, and others in between. I used the bits of information I had gathered to pull more out of her.

Nissa was a smart kid. She had most of the answers and quickly found the ones she hadn't absorbed. It seemed her mind was like a steel trap. If she read it, she remembered it. Her near failure in school had to have been a result of her emotional crisis over her mother's walking out on her.

"That's great, Nissa," I said. "Now what I'd like you to do is write a report on what you learned. Go through each category of training and tell me whether or not it appeals to you and why or why not."

Nissa grinned, the big smile making her freckled face look almost pretty. "This is fun. Not like school at all."

"School should be more like this, but it's difficult when a person has a whole classroom of kids," I said in defense of overworked teachers, something I'd experienced myself in the school where I taught. "Every student needs something different."

"And every teacher isn't as cool as you."

High praise, I thought.

"Though Dawn was pretty neat," Nissa said wistfully.

"You liked her."

"I thought she liked me, too."

"I'm sure she did." I knew she did because Dawn had told me so in more than one of her weekly missives.

"Then why did she leave me?"

A question I would like answered, as well. "Everyone says she eloped."

"I know what they say."

"But you don't believe it?"

"Dawn confided all kinds of stuff in me, but she never said anything about eloping."

"Confided...you mean things about boyfriends?"

Nissa flicked an errant strand of red hair from her forehead. "She told me this guy liked her, but she just said there were lots of fish in the sea."

A guy who liked Dawn...another of her exaggerations or the truth? "This guy—was he someone who works here?"

"Nope. A neighbor. Jack Larson."

Larson...the man who'd been trying to buy one of the stallions. It occurred to me from the exchange I'd overheard that Larson might have been more interested in getting information out of Dawn than he'd been in romancing her.

Not wanting to press Nissa further, I said, "So, back to your assignment…if you need help remembering something, feel free to use the Internet to look it up again."

"That's like taking a test with your book open. Isn't that cheating?"

"Not if I say it isn't. I don't want you to just memorize facts. I want you to learn to think about a topic and know your resources," I explained. "That's how we adults get through real life."

Nissa sighed. "I wish all my teachers could be as cool as you."

And I wished all my students could be as smart as Nissa. Smiling, I watched her work for a few minutes. She seemed so focused. Determined. Like her father. Although, that was the only resemblance I could see between the two. She must look like Priscilla.

The kid was heartbroken at the loss of her mother. I could empathize. What about Damian? I wondered. Was he heartbroken, as well?

My gaze strayed beyond the gazebo to the barn where Damian Graylord was working with a pretty chestnut on a longe line. Rather than watching the horse, I found myself watching the man.

Even from a distance, I could see the muscles of his upper arms flex beneath his shirt, whose sleeves were rolled up above his elbows. He turned with the horse, and my gaze strayed to his thighs, thick and tightly muscled from all the riding he must do. He was beautiful to watch—as graceful as the horse. And his air of command was enough to take away my breath.

Suddenly he seemed to realize I was staring at him. He was too far away from me to actually see if his eyes were focused on me, but I swear I felt them.

Pulse humming, I looked away quickly, turning to his daughter, who was industriously typing away on her laptop. Still, I could feel his gaze on me, the sensation a tangible thing. My heart beat a little too fast for my comfort. And when I heard footsteps and looked up to see him approaching, I could hear the rush of my blood through my head.

"A great day for working outside," he said.

"I thought so. You don't object?"

"Not when my daughter is looking so happy."

Nissa was beaming. "Chloe has me doing this really great project, Dad. I'm learning about the different kinds of horse training."

It was clear that Nissa worshipped her father. And Damian's expression, which softened as he looked at his daughter, told me the feeling was mutual. The close connection between them moved me, and I felt a hunger that I'd put to rest many years before.

"That sounds like a very grown-up assignment, honey," Damian was saying.

"But Nissa is up to it," I quickly assured him. "She's doing a wonderful job."

"Then that calls for a reward. How about a ride after lunch?"

"Chloe can come, too, right?"

Damian fixed his gaze on me and said, "Of course."

"Yay!"

"Unless Chloe doesn't know how to ride," he amended.

"Then I'll teach her."

"And I'll accept any pointers you can give me, Nissa," I said.

I tried not to squirm with discomfort. What was wrong with me? We would be on separate horses, so why was I so reluctant to spend time in Damian's company? That's what I was here to do, after all. Spend time in company with all of them until I learned what had happened to Dawn.

I smiled at Nissa. "I'm sure you're a far better rider than I am."

But it was Damian who answered. "So you do ride."

"Not nearly as often as I would like."

"That won't be a problem here. You can ride daily if you like. The horses always need exercise. I'll pick out a mare that will suit you."

The personal attention was getting to me. "You don't even know what kind of rider I am yet."

"I think I can figure it out." Damian tousled Nissa's already-wild red hair. "Get back to that assignment, young lady."

"I'm on it!"

Nissa's brow furrowed as she picked up where she'd left off before her father had interrupted. I acted as if I had something urgent in my planning book, when in reality I was watching Damian go from the corner of my eye. He looked back once, and either it was my imagination or it really was me rather than Nissa that caught his interest.

If I was right, what was I going to do about it?

LUNCH WAS HEARTIER than I was used to—slices of beef and mashed potatoes with gravy and string beans—but Damian and Alex rose early and worked hard outside, so I expected they needed a meal that stuck to their ribs. I concentrated on my salad and simply tasted everything else. To my amazement Nissa inhaled her meal and asked to be excused so she could change into her new breeches and boots.

"Can I get you seconds, Mr. Damian?" asked a very human-sounding Mrs. Avery.

I did a double take. She was hovering over him, nearly fawning.

"I'm stuffed, but thank you, Mrs. Avery."

"Not too stuffed for dessert, I hope," she said, removing his empty plate. "Merle made one of your favorites. Chocolate flan."

"For lunch? Tell Merle she's spoiling me."

"I shall fetch it for you."

"Cook would do anything for you, bro," Alex said as the housekeeper headed for the kitchen.

It seemed Mrs. Avery would, as well. Wondering if the housekeeper were more like family than hired help—which would explain her possessiveness—I asked, "Has Mrs. Avery worked for your family for a long time?"

"Do you mean did she work for our parents before they retired?" Damian asked. "No."

"Actually, she was Priscilla's creature," Alex said. "But apparently with Priscilla gone, she took to devil-boy."

Priscilla's creature? What an odd way of putting it.

"Only because I pay her salary," Damian said. "Mrs. Avery can be something of an enigma."

"She's an old bat," Alex muttered, as the kitchen door swung open and the housekeeper drifted through carrying a tray.

From the glare she aimed at Alex as she served him his flan, I was pretty certain she'd overheard his comment. As she approached Damian, her expression softened, but I wondered if it was because she liked him—did Mrs. Avery like anyone?—or because, like he'd said, he paid her wages. By the time she got to me, the sour expression was back in place.

I smiled pleasantly in return.

Trading the dining room for the barns couldn't come fast enough for me. At this rate, meals were going to be the low points of my day. We walked out—Alex and me together, Damian following, Nissa having called down that she would be out in a few minutes.

"So you ride, do you?" Alex asked.

"A bit."

"Then perhaps you'll consider riding with me. I could use the company."

"She could never keep up with you," Damian said, sounding annoyed.

"I could hold back for her."

"You never hold back, Alex. That's your problem. You plunge into things without thinking."

Tension between the brothers was rife. But why?

Over me? The idea made my pulse pick up a beat. I remembered wondering if Alex had been interested in Dawn and how Damian would have reacted to that. Then again, Alex might merely be looking for pleasant company on a ride, nothing more. No need to get ahead of myself.

"So what do you say?" Alex asked me directly. "Will you ride with me or will you let big brother keep you from having a good time while you're stuck here?"

"I am not stuck. I chose to be here, remember. Nissa is my priority, but if I am free when you want to ride out, I would consider going along."

"A very well-spoken non-answer."

I laughed. "It's the best I can do for now."

My neck sizzled and I glanced back at Damian, whose gaze seemed to be boring a hole in my flesh. I smiled at him the same way I'd smiled at Mrs. Avery at lunch.

When I turned forward, I saw a slight man in dusty overalls leading a small bay out of the barn.

"There's your ride," Damian said. "Sweet Innocent. She'll be perfect for you."

Sweet Innocent. Was that how he saw me? As in *ingenuous?* Unsophisticated? Harmless? All the better for me to let him think what he would.

"She's beautiful."

If small and seemingly quiet natured, a bit of a disappointment since I was used to riding some feisty mounts. She was also saddled Western, not a problem, though I was used to riding English.

"Clifford, over here," Damian called, indicating he was to give the mare to me. "Alex, come in the barn a minute."

"Uh-oh." Alex wiggled his eyebrows at me. "I think I must have been bad."

I was still laughing when Clifford handed me the reins. He appeared to be fiftyish, with silver threading his thinning brown hair. His face was narrow, his hawkish nose sunburned at the tip.

"Here you go, miss."

"The name's Chloe. Chloe Morgan. I'm Nissa's summer tutor. And you are?"

"Clifford Wakeley—groom, exerciser, hot walker."

"A man of many talents."

"A man who has too much work for too little pay," he groused. "Why Mr. Damian went and hired a schoolteacher he could ill afford instead of giving the rest of us a raise…."

"I'm sorry."

The man shook his head. "Not your fault. You're just another working stiff like me."

The statement gave me reason to probe a bit. I lowered my voice. "So you don't like working for the Graylords?"

"I work for Mr. Damian," he clarified.

"It's a *family* business, though, isn't it?"

"Mr. Alex does promote the place, brings in money. Mares that need to be covered. Buyers. Real enterprising, that Mr. Alex. When he's here, he exercises horses and helps out some, but Mr. Damian runs the farm, makes all the important decisions. At least, he does now."

"He didn't always?" I asked casually, as if it really didn't matter to me.

"Not when his missus was still here." He lowered his voice. "Almost bankrupted the place. She was a selfish woman who deserved whatever she got in the end." Clifford's expression darkened.

"What do you mean, whatever...?"

The groom drew his mouth tight and mumbled, "Miss Nissa's coming. Better get back to my work now."

Nissa was jogging to catch up. I waved to her and she returned the greeting, making me feel good about our first day together. Her attitude was a big departure from what it had been upon my arrival. She was dressed English-style—breeches, flat-heeled boots, hard hat.

"Got to get Wild Cherry!" she yelled, jogging right past me and into the barn as the Graylord brothers exited, Damian leading a big, powerfully built bay.

He was delayed by the blond man I'd seen him with in the pasture earlier—Theo Bosch, barn manager. They seemed to be arguing about something. If only I could read lips....

My mount was getting restless, so I turned to pay her some mind.

"Hey, girl, are you ready to ride?" I murmured, stroking up her long neck and letting my hand rest a minute on her poll, the prominent bony area between her ears.

Then I eased myself in front of her so she could see me and stared deep into warm brown eyes. I stroked the velvet of her muzzle, and as she lipped my hand, I released the treat I'd brought her—a couple of sugar cubes. She nodded her head and snorted in approval.

"Need a leg up?" Alex asked from too close behind me.

He'd startled me—I tried not to let on as I turned to face him. "I'm sure I'll be able to manage."

"I wasn't questioning your skills." He smiled slyly

and winked a hazel eye at me. "What I meant...would you *like* a leg up?"

Emphasis on *like*....

Alex drew close enough that I got a whiff of his subtle aftershave, a fact that made me a little nervous. As did the way he was looking at me, like an after-lunch treat he wanted to savor.

In other circumstances the attention might be flattering, but as it was...I was glad to see Damian coming toward us, his expression set in an ever-familiar scowl.

"Alex, you know Jimmy had to take the day off. The stalls are waiting."

"Clifford can muck them."

"Clifford is exercising one of the mares."

"Theo, then."

"Theo is busy in the tack room."

Alex looked as if he wanted to argue with Damian, but in the end, he clenched his jaw and backed off. If he remembered I was there, I couldn't tell. He stormed toward the barn, throwing a resentful glance over his shoulder at his brother.

Nissa was just coming out of the barn, a chestnut in tow.

"Ready to ride?" Damian asked me.

"As I'll ever be," I said.

Threading my fingers through Sweetie's mane—I'd decided to call her that for short—I slid a booted foot into the stirrup and hiked myself up and onto the mare's back. Then I lifted my left leg and checked the girth one last time—Sweetie had let out the air she'd sucked in and I was able to tighten it another notch.

A clatter of hooves against the earth brought Nissa,

already mounted on Wild Cherry, her gear English rather than Western, even with me and Sweetie.

Then Damian mounted in one smooth movement, his body in motion a thing of beauty to admire. His horse was already moving before he even had his right leg over the saddle.

"Follow me."

Anywhere, I thought, acknowledging the quickened pace of my pulse.

I always felt this way when I rode, but something told me there was more to my excitement than being on the back of a horse.

Nissa followed her father, and I followed her, glancing over my shoulder briefly as I moved off.

Alex was standing outside the barn, staring after us. I couldn't quite catch his expression, but I didn't think he was smiling.

So what was going on between the two brothers? Somehow I felt caught in the middle…and wondered if the same thing might have happened to Dawn….

Chapter Five

No matter that Centaur had died in that area, Damian led the way out to the palisades. There the view would be magnificent, stretching across the Mississippi River seemingly forever. Odd how something could be so beautiful and yet so ugly at the same time. The memories were ugly…thankfully they didn't touch Nissa. She knew what had happened here, but she hadn't seen anything. Nothing to give her more nightmares.

Priscilla had given her enough of those.

Collecting Sarge, he held the stallion back and turned him in a circle so that Nissa could take the lead, while he would bring up the rear.

"Is something wrong?" Chloe asked as he approached.

"Just giving my daughter a nudge in the right direction." He wanted Nissa to remain as fearless as she had been on the day she'd been born.

"She seems at home on a horse."

"As well she should."

And as did Chloe herself, Damian realized after riding behind her for a few minutes. Unusual for a city girl. Then again, Dawn Reed had been a city girl and nearly as comfortable on a horse as Chloe. Perhaps the horses were the very thing that had drawn both women from the city.

"Dad?" Nissa called, glancing back at him.

He gave her the signal to go ahead and she urged Cherry into a faster gait. His attention was immediately drawn to Chloe's saddle that cradled her nicely rounded derriere. No bouncing at all—she sat the saddle easily.

Damian waited to see how she would do when Nissa slowed to take them down to the river via a series of switchback curves and a few areas where the slope was excessive. Chloe seemed a bit nervous but didn't make one wrong move.

When they reached the riverbank and the horses sloshed in the shallows, he drew up alongside her. "I'm impressed."

She laughed. "That I haven't fallen off? Wait…the ride isn't over yet."

"That a city girl is so comfortable on a horse."

A becoming flush filled her cheeks and she looked away, mumbling, "I guess I was born to ride or something," then signaled Sweet Innocence to move ahead.

Odd that she would avoid talking about her riding skills. Why? It was obvious that she'd been trained and had spent a lot of time on a horse's back. Her reluctance to discuss her proficiency put him on alert. He wanted to know what else she was keeping to herself.

A horn blasted from the paddleboat on the other side of the river, the haunting sound jarring Damian because it reminded him of Centaur's death. He could hear those foghorns all the way to the house. They weren't far from where the stallion had crashed against the rocks.

For a moment, he saw again the chainsaw-armed crew that had come to retrieve the dead horse.

Nissa's shriek of laughter as she raced Cherry along the water's edge startled Damian back to the present.

"Your daughter is certainly enjoying herself," Chloe said, her voice warm with approval. "When did she learn to ride?"

"From the time she could sit a horse in front of me." Damian couldn't hide his pride. "She's a natural."

"She wants to be just like her father."

Damian shifted uneasily in the saddle. "Nissa is her own person."

"But she wants to work with horses, to train them. Obviously, she gets that ambition from you."

To change the subject he said, "And here I was hoping she would go for something more sensible."

"What would be more sensible to you?"

"An astrophysicist?"

Chloe laughed. "I think Nissa is as far from that particular occupation as she can get."

Thinking about the mounting bills he couldn't pay, wanting his daughter to inherit something better than a lifetime of worry, Damian sighed. "I know. It's just that this business is so uncertain, even when you have top horses and the best clients."

Chloe's sympathetic gaze caught him for a moment. Damian was mesmerized. Every time he was around the tutor, he felt inexplicably drawn to her. He hadn't felt that way about any woman before. Not even about Priscilla.

And then Nissa shouted, "Dad, let's take the north trail back up!" jerking him out of the trance.

He waved her on and picked up the pace a bit to catch up. No matter how good a rider Nissa was, she was still a kid and he didn't want to let her out of his sight. Chloe stayed right with him.

"How many horses do you have on the property?" she asked.

"Have on the property or own?"

"You don't own them all?"

"Nope. At the moment, three studs belong to the farm. And seven of the broodmares. Another ten mares were brought here to be covered by the studs. Impregnated," he explained, guiding Sarge onto the trail that would take them up. "They'll stay at least for a while after they deliver a live foal. Some will be here longer because the owners want us to start training their colts and fillies. We have a couple of yearlings and a juvenile who'll be boarded here until they're sold. And then we have our personal horses," he said, indicating Sarge and Cherry. "And a few retirees."

"So that makes…"

Halfway back to the top of the bluff, Damian said, "Presently, thirty-one of various ages."

"Wow, that's a lot of work taking care of so many horses."

"Especially since most of them are used to being exercised on a track every day. Or, for the young ones—they need to get used to doing so."

"Surely you don't ride every one of those horses every day?"

He shook his head. "Impossible. They get pastured and are lucky if they get worked out once a week."

Damian wondered if he should read more than simple interest in Chloe's curiosity.

When they were on solid ground, high above the river, she asked, "So has this always been Graylord Pastures?"

"Only for the last hundred and twenty years or so. Most of it, anyway. My dad picked up one small property when the owner retired and his kids didn't want to work the place. And when I took over the business, I picked up another farm that was going bankrupt." Irony of ironies, considering his own current circumstances. "Actually, Bosch Barns was a riding outfit, customers being mostly tourists from Galena. The high price of insurance killed the business."

"Bosch? As in Theo?"

"Right. The place belonged to Theo's father. He got himself a small place in Savanna and a part-time job working in a local shop. Theo came to work for me."

As he might soon have to work for someone else if his luck didn't change.

Despite his reassurances to Nissa earlier today, Damian really didn't know that the farm would be all right. If things kept going sour as they had been, he could be forced out. Then what? Horses were all he knew. He would have to go to work for someone else, which could mean dragging Nissa around the country. No life for a kid.

As if the weather were affected by his quickly changing mood, dark clouds began to roll across the sky. More rain was predicted to be on its way, but it wasn't due until late that night.

Nissa was scooting through the stand of trees ahead. Chloe suddenly stopped her mare and stared.

"Is something wrong?" Damian asked, stopping and circling Sarge to come alongside her.

"That's where it happened."

His gut tightened as Damian turned his gaze to the trees and Nissa. "*What* happened?"

"Last night," Chloe said. "I was heading through the stand toward the house when I heard noises. I turned to see that gray horse ride out of the mists along the bluff straight for me."

All that was left of Damian's good humor evaporated in a heartbeat.

TENSION WIRED OFF DAMIAN like a tangible thing. His mercurial mood swept through me, leaving me with little breath. I wanted to demand a reason for the mood swing, but I feared it was my fault for bringing up the horse.

Nissa had gone ahead of us. The only thing that kept me from speeding to catch up to her was that the house and barns came into view. The horses needed to be walked out before being reinstated in their stalls. Thanking the fact that I could see the house and barns ahead, I told myself to remain calm and pretend nothing was wrong.

I'd meant to talk to Damian about Nissa's sleepwalking, but I'd missed my opportunity, and obviously this wasn't the right time. The conversation could wait until he was in a better mood.

Nissa was leading her horse into the barn by the time we caught up to her. She waved and kept going.

Dismounting, I said, "Well, that was a wonderful treat," as if the afternoon hadn't soured. The sun hid behind a bank of clouds, and the wind was picking up.

Suddenly beside me, Damian demanded, "What were you thinking, bringing up the damn horse again?"

"I don't see the harm—"

"The harm would be in upsetting Nissa with talk of death and ghosts. You know how fragile she's been emotionally. The last thing she needs to hear is some drivel that would set her off again!"

Somewhere in that diatribe I gasped and my mouth gaped, but that hadn't stopped Damian from continuing his rant. I didn't even think before responding in kind.

"I merely told you that I saw a horse and it nearly ran me over. You're the one who labeled it a ghost!"

As I spoke up for myself, his eyes widened. *Uh-oh.* Now I'd gone and done it, let my temper best me.

"And I told you there is no horse fitting your description on the property, nor in the immediate vicinity."

"Then perhaps it got loose somewhere farther down the road and made its way here!"

"There is no bloody horse!" His visage dark, he held out his horse's reins and said, "Take him."

I almost did until I realized Damian wasn't talking to me. Theo had come up behind me. He took Sarge's reins, and Damian stalked off.

"I'll take your horse, as well, miss."

"Are you sure—?"

"Damian will want you to get back to the girl."

Realizing he hadn't put the "Mr." before Damian, as had the other servants, I figured the barn manager was on a different footing with him. Well, of course Theo must be, considering the circumstance. He'd been another landowner until the family business had gone sour.

"Yes, of course," I said, handing Sweetie's reins to Theo.

"A word of advice, miss?"

"About?"

"Thwarting Damian. Don't."

My heart skipped a beat at the warning. "You make it sound like he's dangerous to cross."

"You could say that," he muttered, checking the horses as if to make sure they were cool enough before turning them toward the nearby water trough.

I stood there stunned for a moment. And felt chilled through by the wind that swept across the open area. What had Theo meant by that? Was he simply referring to Damian's quick temper or something darker?

Had *Dawn* crossed Damian?

I went after the barn manager, figuring this was an opportune moment to learn something more about my employer. "Theo, wait a minute."

He stopped and turned toward me, not appearing in the least surprised. "Yes, miss?"

"What did you mean by that? Damian's being dangerous to cross? He's not a violent man…is he?"

"Not that anyone's proved."

My mouth went dry. "Please…?"

"You'll hear it from someone, sooner or later, so it might as well be me. His wife disappeared under mysterious circumstances."

"I thought they were divorced," I choked out.

"That's *his* story. But no one here has seen Priscilla since the night she mysteriously disappeared."

I would have tried to get more out of him, but just

then Nissa left the barn. Frustrated, I nodded at Theo. He moved the horses to the nearby water trough.

"So how did you like the ride?" the girl asked as she jogged over to me.

"It was great. You're such an accomplished rider."

Nissa grinned. "Dad taught me. Who taught you?"

"I took lessons this last year."

Her grin faded. "Like Dawn. She said the same thing."

I clenched my jaw hard. Now why had I told her a truth that could come back to bite me? I should have fudged a bit, made it sound as if I'd been riding for ages.

Hoping to distract her from thinking about the coincidence, I said, "When we get back in the house, you'll have enough time to clean up and to write in your journal before dinner."

I glanced back and noticed that Theo was watching us. Had he heard, as well?

"I know just what I'm going to write about," Nissa announced.

With that she skipped ahead, leaving me to my thoughts as I approached the house alone.

Dark thoughts about Damian.

About Priscilla's disappearance…

…which sounded too similar to Dawn's disappearance to be discounted.

I never had believed my friend would have eloped without telling me—at least she would have let me know after the fact if not before.

Damian had said she'd written the note on the computer in the library. I wondered if the file had been erased or if it was still accessible. I also wondered how I could access it without arousing anyone's suspicions. Everyone knew I had my laptop with me, and the Internet connection was wireless, so there was no reason I would need to use the library computer.

I would find a way....

But what about Priscilla? a little voice whispered. If no one had seen her since the night in question, maybe she really was dead as Nissa had claimed.

I didn't know what to believe, not about Dawn, not about Damian's ex-wife.

Not even about the ghost horse or why Damian had been nearly apoplectic about my mentioning it.

How did they all connect together? I wondered. Would I ever find out?

I THOUGHT DINNER MIGHT BE a laborious affair, but Damian was mellow. For him. He raptly listened to his daughter go on and on about horse training until I thought it was a pose.

"It sounds like you had a good day," he said, sounding completely sincere.

"A great day, Dad."

"So how will you follow it up tomorrow?" This was addressed to me.

"I thought Nissa could research the types of horses and do a report on the difference between breeds."

"And you're qualified to know whether or not the report is accurate?"

I heard the challenge in his words. "This isn't a test. It's an exploration. I'm sure I'll learn a lot from Nissa's report. The idea is for *her* to learn how to access information she needs and to give her options on how to use that information."

"So you want to teach her to think for herself?"

"Exactly."

"She has an excellent example for that, doesn't she?"

For a moment I thought he meant himself, then I realized he was referring to me. To my standing up for myself. The flush that filled my cheeks irritated me. I didn't want to be susceptible to the man.

But there it was.

Alex sat at the table taking it all in. Even now he was watching us through hooded eyes. But whatever he was thinking, he was playing it close to the vest, so to speak. Tonight he was watching…waiting…but for what?

My growing discomfort became unbearable. I needed to get away from everyone in this house and have some time to myself to think.

Rising, I placed my cloth napkin next to my plate. "If you'll excuse me."

"You're leaving before dessert?" Nissa sounded horrified at the thought.

"I couldn't eat another bite. Truly." I faced Damian and asked, "Just to be clear, I do have my evenings to myself, do I not?"

"Of course. Feel free to do whatever pleases you."

"Good. I'll do just that."

What would please me now would be another walk, one that would take me away from the house and its inhabitants.

The weather was driving in on the area. The sky had

grown darker than it should have been at this time of the evening, and the wind attacked the house in gusts. I grabbed a flashlight, but, certain that I would make it back to the house before the storm, which wasn't due until the wee hours of the morning, I passed on the umbrella.

I'm not sure what I intended when I set out, but I must have had a subconscious wish to find proof that I hadn't been seeing things the night before, because as I entered the stand of trees between the house and the river, I sought the area where I'd seen the gray horse.

Pretty sure I'd found it, I flashed the light along the ground. I didn't know if I would actually find any prints since the storm had even penetrated the trees. Then the beam picked up an object that didn't belong—the flashlight that I'd dropped the night before. I picked it up and put it in my pocket and checked the ground more carefully.

Just there…a footprint…one of mine.

Encouraged, I widened my search and caught a few impressions made by me.

But none that had been made by a horse.

I didn't understand. If the rain hadn't been severe enough here to wash out everything, why was it I couldn't I find any prints in the shape of a horseshoe?

No matter what Damian said, my imagination hadn't been playing tricks on me.

Maybe I ought to let it go. Seeing a horse that wasn't supposed to exist didn't have anything to do with Dawn's disappearance, the only reason I was here. I couldn't let my pique, first at being laughed at, then at being yelled at, distract me from my purpose.

I was thinking about giving up what seemed like a

futile search and returning to the house when I heard what I swore was an equine snort from somewhere behind me.

My heart skipped a beat and I whirled around and stared hard through the trees. No movement other than the mist licking the ground. The air had cooled fast, which meant fog was sure to follow. The small forested area was already turning spooky again.

Still…I couldn't help myself. I edged forward in the direction from which the noise had come. My breathing shallow, I crept on silent feet and listened intently for a repeat of that distinctive sound.

There it came again!

I traveled faster now, my pulse drumming, my excitement growing as I heard the distinctive sound yet a third time. I broke into the clearing near the bluffs fully expecting to see my mystery horse awaiting me.

Nothing.

I whistled, keeping the sound low and soft and nonthreatening. Head turning, eyes skimming every inch of open space, I moved across the expanse, careful not to go too far lest I be fooled by the fog and take a tumble down the palisades.

Like Centaur…a chilling thought.

A soft whinny spun me around and I saw the gray horse standing near the forest edge, soft, dark eyes fixed on me. I moved forward. Rather than away, the horse circled me, the equine dance studied, until we had nearly reversed positions. Then the gray threw up its head and whinnied again as it clacked a hoof against rock over and over and over.

What the heck was he doing? I couldn't tell. I moved closer. The fog twisted up the long gray legs and around the big body, nearly engulfing the horse. Still those eyes stared at me, as if willing me to come see…what?

As I drew close enough to touch the beast, it backed off, head bobbing.

So I flashed my light at the rock. I stooped to take a closer look and saw something sparkle from a crack. I glanced back to see what the horse was doing, but like the night before, it had vanished. A sense of foreboding filled me as I reached for the object and pulled it free.

One look at the exquisite silver Celtic design interlaced with pieces of topaz and my knees gave way. Gasping, my heart pounding, I fell to the ground without ever taking my eyes from the object in my hand.

I curled my fingers around the direct connection to my dearest friend and couldn't stop the cry that escaped my lips.

THE SUMMER TUTOR was going to be a problem. That had been obvious from the first. Now here she was at the bluffs—again!—as if drawn to this very spot by a ghost.

She'd picked up something.

What?

From the forested area looking out, it was too far to see the object in her hand. What would even compel her to look for something in this fog?

And why the hell was she crying?

Her head hung and her shoulders jerked and she swiped a hand at her eyes. It took her a moment, but she got hold of herself, stood and slipped the object into her pants pocket. She looked around and shuddered.

The incident was enough to set anyone on edge. No doubt about it, Chloe Morgan was bad news.

Question was…what to do about her?

Chapter Six

I walk through fog-shrouded forest, my heart in my throat…searching…always searching.

Searching for answers…

Searching for the truth…

Searching for Dawn.

A pale shadow sideswipes me, nearly knocking me over.

Pay attention!

I absorb the words without a voice and I know they concern my friend. My heart thunders in my chest. What am I missing? What don't I see that I should?

I seek the shadow, catch up to it. The pale horse. Our gazes connect and I am filled with a surety that it wants something of me. Or perhaps for me.

But what?

Then I see her…there all the time. She steps from behind the horse and reaches out to me.

"Dawn? Where have you been?" I ask.

She doesn't answer.

I glance down at her outstretched hand. Cradled in her palm is the hair clip. She offers it to me and looks at me as if I should know what this means….

My eyes flashed open and a pale shadow teased me from the corner of the room. I turned sleep-heavy eyes to see the curtains flailing. The storm had hit. Rain drummed overhead. I rose to lower the windows, but before doing so, my pulse fluttering in anticipation, I looked out over the grounds.

No matter how hard or how far I searched, I saw nothing resembling a pale-hided horse.

I returned to my bed and sat on the edge and turned on the table light. The dull pool illuminated the nightstand and the hair clip that lay on its surface. I stared at it for a moment—the fancy hair clip whose Celtic design matched the one she'd had tattooed around her wrist. I'd bought it the year before from an artist who had assured me it was one of a kind.

My birthday present to Dawn.

She'd loved this hair ornament. She would never have dropped it and not gone back to find it.

And why was it at the bluffs?

I had trouble believing Dawn would have voluntarily gone near the palisades. She was afraid both of heights and—since she'd never learned to swim—of any body of water.

More and more convinced that something terrible had happened to my friend, I wondered how I could prove it.

The note!

I checked the time—barely five—surely too early an hour for anyone else to be awake. This was it, my opportunity to get to the computer in the library without anyone knowing.

I thought to change out of the lace-trimmed cotton

nightgown and put on some shoes, but in the end chose not to waste the time. If I hurried, I could be in and out of the library in minutes and with no one the wiser.

I cracked open my door. Night-lights glowed softly, one at the landing, the other at the bottom of the stairs. I listened hard. No sound but the rain, which seemed to be slowing. Nissa's door was closed and not a sound came from her room, so I assumed the girl was still safely tucked in bed as she had been earlier when I'd checked on her. As far as I could tell, not a creature was stirring anywhere in the house....

Shallow breaths, I told myself, slipping into the hall and making my way down the steps, careful to remain as silent as a ghost. Reaching the first floor without being discovered, I took a deep, shaky breath and tried to relax. My knees were wobbly, and I could feel my heartbeat as it thumped against the wall of my chest.

Gliding through the night-lit hall like a wraith made me think of a dozen rental movies Dawn and I had watched together, hunkered down in our living room and sharing microwaved popcorn. Thrillers, horror movies—young heroines risking their lives to save the day.

I stopped at the library door, which was shut. I pressed my ear to the wooden panel but heard nothing that would indicate anyone was inside. I glanced at the bottom of the door but no light escaped the gap.

A swallow for courage allowed me to turn the handle, then to let myself into the room.

The rain had stopped during my flight down the staircase, and the moon had come out from behind the clouds. A chill blue light swept through the room, and as my eyes adjusted, I could see that it was empty. The smell of charred wood lingered, and I wondered if the scent came from a recent fire or from the one Damian and I had shared.

The last caught me, and for a moment I was filled with thoughts of my too-compelling employer. In my mind's eye, I could see the potency of his every feature, the thickness of his dark hair… I could feel the strength of his arms, the rock-hard solidness of his body.

My own flesh quivered in response.

The attraction for me was strong. So was the doubt. Part of me—unreasonably, perhaps—wanted to know why Damian Graylord hadn't delved into an investigation of an employee's disappearance himself. If he knew something more than I, he was keeping the knowledge close.

Damian was no one to trust, not until he proved himself.

I moved to the desk and turned the work lamp on low and then—praying it didn't require some identification or password—fired up the computer.

My nerves were on edge as I waited for the various programs to load. The process seemed to take forever before the electronic noises stopped, the screen stabilized and the computer hummed steadily. I brought up the word-processing program. No passwords. I heaved a sigh of relief.

And then I noted the large number of folders—each with subfolders—and wondered how the heck I was going to find one lonely little file when I didn't even know the file name. I scanned the contents of dozens of folders before it hit me that I could do this automatically. I clicked on the system's search program and entered

"Dawn," since Damian had said the note had been "signed" with her typed rather than written name.

The search took only a moment. Several documents came up. I changed the view so I could see "details" that included dates and chose the latest entry.

My pulse surged when I realized I'd found it. Quickly, I read the short missive.

> Dear Damian:
> It's been great working for you, but I met a man on one of my trips into Galena. He swept me off my feet and wants me to marry him. My things are packed and I'm waiting for him now. We're eloping. By tomorrow I'll be married.
> Goodbye.
>
> Dawn

I printed out the message. For good measure, I called up my Web-mail account and forwarded a copy of the note in an e-mail to myself. And then I read it again.

The missive didn't sit right with me. Dawn was impulsive, yes…and yet this forthright explanation didn't sound anything like her. She was a gusher. She liked to tell you all the details. To embellish. She hadn't mentioned the name of the man she was to marry, not even a first name, just as I'd been told. And she hadn't so much as mentioned Nissa. I knew she cared about the girl, and I didn't believe she would walk away without at least asking Damian to say goodbye for her.

I would swear Dawn didn't write this. I closed the file and took a look at the others called up by the search. Just letters having to do with hiring her. About to shut down the computer, I blinked at that list of "details" about the files, and one thing connected with Dawn's goodbye jumped out at me. The date—5/21/05—that was the day *after* Dawn disappeared.

I was still trying to absorb the disparity when, from somewhere in the house, I heard a noise, as if someone were moving around....

My fingers flew over the keys, commanding first the word-processing program to close down, then the operating system. All the while I could hardly breathe. I listened for another noise that might indicate that a person was approaching, but either there was nothing to hear or the computer program shutting down was loud enough to cover.

Just in case, I turned off the desk lamp and prayed as I folded the copy of Dawn's supposed farewell and slipped it into the pocket of my nightgown.

Outside, thunder rumbled ominously, the sky lit and split, leaving me startled and sweating. Once more, rain drummed against the house.

Finally the screen before me went dark. I clicked off the monitor and wished I could do the same to the printer to snuff the ready light. Its tiny green glow mocked me. But if I turned off the printer, Damian would know for certain someone had been messing with his computer.

So I let it be and prayed fate was with me as I stepped toward the door. Again I put my ear to the wooden panel. Again, nothing.

Thankful my luck was holding, I left the library the way I'd entered—silently. Even so, the hairs on my arms rose. Something didn't feel right.

I began my escape, but halfway down the hall I caught another sound like that of a shoe against wood, only I couldn't tell from which direction it came.

Another scuff shuddered down my spine and pushed me faster. I intended to go right past the staircase and into the kitchen to hide. I was nearly there when a shove in the middle of my back sent me flying. I tried to catch myself, but my feet tangled on something soft and I went down, my head connecting with something hard.

Light flared behind my eyes…then faded fast….

"CHLOE, CAN YOU HEAR ME?"

The deep rumble entered my head and forced me up out of an unnatural slumber.

"Chloe, open your eyes and say something."

I blinked my eyes open to meet Damian's frown. All I said was, "I'm still alive," as if it was a surprise to me. Which in a way it was, I guess.

I thought the rain had stopped again because early-morning light crept from the hall window to illuminate Damian hovering over me.

How long had I been out?

"I didn't want to move you in case anything was broken."

So he'd left me in a heap on the floor, where apparently I'd tripped over a scatter rug. Vaguely I remembered thinking someone had shoved me. Did it really happen or had my imagination been working overtime? It *was* possible that I'd simply been clumsy in my haste to hide after hearing those noises. I simply wasn't certain.

I tested my limbs. "I think everything is working."

"Let me help you up."

Damian slid an arm around my waist and lifted. I was on my feet in seconds. He didn't let go. Warmth shuddered through me as I realized all that stood between me and him was a thin cotton shift on my part, a thin cotton T-shirt on his. He seemed to realize it, too. His gaze intensified as did his grip on me. His long fingers biting into my flesh made me warm all over, and for a moment—watching his face draw near—I thought he was going to kiss me. The idea made my heart flutter.

He looked deep into my eyes, no doubt to see if the pupils were even. "How is your head?"

"Hard," I muttered, biting down my disappointment.

A smile quivered along his lips. "I already knew that. But does it hurt? Are you dizzy? Seeing double?"

"I think I'm okay. You can let me go now."

"'Think' isn't good enough."

He kept his arm around me as he swept me down the hall, and for a moment I thought he might lift me into his arms and carry me up the stairs.

And then I realized where he was headed.

Good Lord, was he really taking me to the library? How much time *had* passed? I wondered frantically. Surely enough so the printer-ready light would be off.

When Damian threw open the door, he didn't give me time to check. He whirled me around, saying, "Sit."

My legs were back against one of the chairs in front of the fireplace. I sat.

"Stay," he added, before disappearing out of the room again.

Sit...stay...? Did I look like a dog?

For all I knew, I might. I put a hand to my forehead, wondering exactly where I'd smacked it and what I'd smacked it against. My fingers slid into my hairline before I winced. I felt something lumpy and warm and sticky, and when I took my hand away, my fingertips were red.

Now I felt dizzy.

"I can fix you up," Damian said as he came back into the room, "but I'm not a doctor."

"I don't need a doctor."

"We'll see how bad that cut is and how you feel when you have to stand on your own."

He'd brought a first-aid kit. He opened it on a side table and took out a square packet which he proceeded to rip open.

"I'll be gentle," he promised, pushing aside hair to get to the cut.

Gentle or not made no difference. The antiseptic burned. I tried not to wince.

"Swear if you have to," he muttered, turning the pad and applying it a second time.

"Ladies don't swear."

"Did your mother teach you that? It's a lie."

"All right, then, *I* don't swear." At least not aloud. I was doing plenty of silent cursing as Damian tended to the head wound.

He pulled a bigger packet out of the kit, ripped it open and twisted the smaller bag inside. "Cold pack," he explained. "It'll keep the swelling down."

I grimaced as I touched it to the lump on my head.

Damian picked up a small flashlight and switched it on. Then he cupped my chin and tilted my head and shone the light into my eyes—first one, then the other.

"Will I live?" I asked.

"Most definitely. Both eyes respond to the light equally, so it doesn't look like you have a concussion. I would still prefer you see a doctor this morning. We can be at the hospital in Galena in twenty minutes."

I had a feeling he would nag me to death until I agreed to something. "A doctor but no emergency room." I'd had enough of hospitals before my mother died.

"Doc Haggerty won't be in until eight."

Which was probably two hours away. "It'll take me that long to get ready to go."

Damian flicked an eyebrow at me. "I see you believe in the art of compromise."

"Survival instinct," I said, laughing, then regretting it when my head began to throb.

"Did some survival instinct bring you downstairs in the middle of the night?"

I thought quickly for a way to excuse my being out of my room. "I was heading for the kitchen to get that dessert I missed at dinner."

His look grew penetrating, as if he could get inside me. Because he didn't believe me?

"I can get dessert for you now."

"Thanks, but no. The moment has passed."

"So what happened exactly."

Exactly? I didn't really know. Someone had been behind me, had pushed me…but for all I knew, it could have been Damian. Not that I really believed it. Still, I wasn't going to tell him anything more than I had to. Even if he was guilty of nothing, he was my employer, and if he knew what I was up to, he would undoubtedly fire me pronto and send me packing.

"It was dark. I didn't see the rug." I had a hard time lying, so I stuck to the truth as closely as I could. "I tripped." All true.

My story sounded good. So why didn't Damian look convinced? Warmth flushed my cheeks, but I held his gaze waiting for the questioning to continue. In the end he nodded and held out a hand.

"Let's see how you feel when you stand up."

I set down the cold pack. Not wanting renewed physical contact, I used both hands on the arms of the chair. I stood on my own and turned my head slowly to see if the room would spin with it. My equilibrium seemed just fine.

"No dizziness."

"Let's get you to your room, then." Damian held out his arm. "Hang on to me."

He gave me no choice. As much as I didn't want to, I felt it was simpler to hook my hand around his arm. I tried not to think about it, but the touch of his bare flesh got to me. The warmth spread along my fingers and down my arm and continued on until it reached my bare toes.

I took an unsteady step and fell against Damian. Suddenly his arms were around me again, and his face was so close to mine that his breath laved my cheek. Self-consciously looking into his eyes, I saw heat there that warmed me through. His lips parted…drew closer…stopped within a fraction of mine.

"Are you all right?"

The words sounded a bit choked. Just the way I felt. I felt other things, too. Beneath the soft nightgown, my nipples tightened and the heat of his body pierced me. For a moment all I could think about was his body tangled with mine in a rhythm that would bring me to the brink of madness.

I pushed against the idea, pushed against him physically so that I could breathe again. "I'm steady now."

"Good," he growled, not sounding at all pleased.

Perhaps he'd had like thoughts of kissing me, touching me, taking me.... Thankfully he put them aside somehow and became all business as he led me out of the library. He took it slow, especially on the staircase—torture—and I was relieved to reach my room.

"I want you to lie down. Just take it easy for a while. I'll get an ice pack for your head and leave a message with the doc. Maybe we can get you in before hours."

The moment I closed the door between us, I heaved a sigh of relief. It was hard to think straight with Damian so close. Quickly I changed into a pair of navy pants and a blue shirt. The nightgown made me too vulnerable in his presence. I fetched the printout from my pocket and hid it in one of my cases, after which I made the bed. By then my head was throbbing like mad, so I crawled on top of the covers.

A moment later there was a knock at my door.

Damian....

Hoping I seemed composed, I said, "Come in."

But it wasn't Damian who entered. Her expression disapproving as it always seemed to be when she looked my way, Mrs. Avery marched into the room and presented me with an ice pack.

"Mr. Damian said you needed this for your head."

Hoping she would just leave, I took the ice pack from her and said, "Thank you."

"Humph. You wouldn't be putting people in this house to such trouble if only you would stay put at night."

"I'm sorry if you feel inconvenienced."

"You'll be sorrier if you don't keep your nose where it belongs."

Was that a threat?

Before I could ask, Mrs. Avery was in the hall closing my door.

That sure *sounded* like a threat.

I put the ice pack to my head and winced. But the pain only distracted me from my dark thoughts for a moment.

Had Mrs. Avery heard me leave my room and followed me? Had I indeed been pushed and was she the one who'd done it? I knew she didn't like me, but what reason would she have to harm me?

Unless...

Impossible. She couldn't know who I was or what I was doing here...

Could she?

Chapter Seven

To both my disappointment and my relief, Damian didn't take me to see Doc Haggerty, who checked me out thoroughly and sent me on my way with instructions to turn on a light the next time I decided to take a nighttime stroll.

As if he were trying to avoid me, Damian had passed on the honor of escorting me to town to his brother. At least I wasn't on edge the whole time. Alex Graylord was charming and flirtatious as always—the exact opposite of his brooding older brother.

"We should do this more often," Alex said as we left the first-floor office in the doctor's house, a big place at the edge of Savanna.

"What? Have me smack my head so you can drive me to see a doctor to make sure I didn't scramble my brains?"

Alex laughed and opened the car door for me. "Not exactly. I was talking about spending some time together, away from that place."

That place...is that how he thought of Graylord Pastures, like it was something he wanted to avoid?

Alex was certainly handsome as sin, and charming—definitely the easier of the brothers to be around—but I didn't want to give him any ideas about my being available. The last thing I needed at the moment was romance of any sort.

I said, "I haven't even settled in yet."

"No reason you need to settle," he countered. "It'll be time to pack up and go back to Chicago before you know."

"A lot can happen in ten weeks." Hopefully that was enough time to find out what had happened to Dawn.

"True," Alex said, starting the engine. "But you might as well make the experience as painless for yourself as possible."

He kept his voice light but I felt his tension. Unless I was reading him wrong, he wasn't finding it painless to work for the family business. Then why didn't he simply leave, or at least work at something else that would make him happier?

Not wanting to lose my big opportunity to get some information out of Alex, I changed the conversation, fast. "I think I've upset your brother."

"Not hard to do. What does devil-boy have himself in a twist over now?"

"This is kind of weird…but the other night when I went for that walk down to the bluffs, I saw a gray horse. Damian insisted that was impossible."

"A gray horse? By the bluffs?"

Realizing Alex's tone had changed, I delved right in. "He told me a horse had died there. No details."

"It was a real tragedy in more ways than one."

"I don't understand."

"Centaur's death may have spelled the death of Graylord Pastures. Actually, the real cause is financial distress, this being one more nail in the financial coffin."

"Surely Centaur was insured."

"*Was* being the operative word. Priscilla never got around to paying that last and all-important premium."

The words "How irresponsible" were out of my mouth before I could contain them.

Stopped at the last intersection before hitting open road, Alex glanced at me, eyebrows raised. "No kidding. Priscilla bought Centaur in the first place, not caring his purchase tanked the budget. She said we would make up the inflated six-figure price in stud fees."

"But the stallion died before you could recoup."

"Damian wasn't going to keep him long enough to find out. He had him on the market…not that anyone was jumping to shell out a quarter of a million in this economy."

"Couldn't you have waited awhile?" I asked.

Alex shook his head. "The farm had suffered too much bad luck, and the books were already looking shabby. The past year has been unbelievable. A barn burned, tractor breakdowns, a downed fence and valuable animals on the loose…then, even though the horses were all right, losing a top client…all combined to put the farm in the red."

A horn blaring behind us jerked Alex out of his explanation. He put the car in motion, and it took off from the crossroad with a squeal of tires.

"It must be very hard to keep a business going these days."

"I suggested Damian think about selling before there was nothing left to sell, but as usual he ignored me. My brother won't leave the land until they drag him out kicking and screaming." He muttered, "Now if only we could find the Equine Diamonds, everyone could be happy."

"Equine Diamonds?" I echoed.

"Legendary gemstones—the prize for a match race. This was back in the 1890s. An ancestor bet the farm against a bag of diamonds, that her horse was faster than that of her chief competitor. Her horse won."

"And the diamonds?"

"Lost. Great-great-great-grandma Anna hid them someplace for safekeeping, because she never sold them. When she died, she left them to her sons in her will but didn't reveal the hidey-hole. Maybe she thought looking for a purple velvet bag filled with uncut diamonds worth only-God-knows-how-much would keep them here forever."

"If the diamonds even existed in the first place."

"They *did* exist. There are newspaper accounts of the match race and the prize."

An interesting tale, possibly no more. The dead horse was all too real. I circled back to that topic. "So how did Centaur fall to his death?"

"Simple. He was terrified of thunderstorms. One came up in the middle of the night. The stallion freaked and got loose."

I thought Alex wanted to say more, but he didn't. "So Centaur headed for the bluffs in a state of panic."

"Unfortunately for him…and for the business."

Throughout, Alex had talked about Graylord Pastures in a disconnected way, as if it were an entity of which he had no part. Indeed, from what he'd told me, it seemed Alex would be willing to leave the place, unlike his brother.

Was Damian such a strong personality that he would make his brother feel left out? Or was that a foolish question?

"Where exactly did Centaur fall to his death?" I asked.

"Right where you come out of the woods, opposite the clearing."

My mind raced as I looked in that general direction—we were less than a mile from the entrance to Graylord Pastures. "So close. That's the very area where I saw him—the gray horse." And where I'd found Dawn's hair clip. "Damian joked about my seeing a ghost horse. Maybe he wasn't so far from the truth."

I expected Alex to laugh at me the way Damian had at first, only he didn't. He seemed a bit tense and changed the subject so fast it made my head spin.

What was it that made both Graylord brothers shy away from the topic?

"I THINK WE SHOULD make this a short morning, considering your head injury and all," Nissa said halfway through her tutoring session.

"The morning is short enough as it is." The girl made a face that told me she hadn't really expected to talk me into it. She was merely testing me. "So what have you found so far?" I asked.

Nissa gave me a brief verbal survey of the horses of

the world, then we talked a bit about what attracted her in a horse. I realized she'd absorbed every word when listening to her father and the other men who worked the place. She seemed to know everything there was to know about lineage, conformation and color.

"Chestnuts are my favorite," Nissa said. "But I like grays next best."

Chestnuts being a given, considering Wild Cherry was her personal horse.

"Why grays?"

"You don't see them so much. We have mostly bays around here."

"Right." As Damian had informed me, no one in the vicinity had a gray horse.

"We did have a gray." Nissa sighed, the sound sad. "But he had a terrible death."

"I'm sure he's gone to horse heaven."

"Uh-uh. He's still around." She lowered her voice. "Don't tell Dad I said so—he'd be mad again—but I saw him."

"Saw?" So I wasn't the only one who'd seen a gray horse? "When?"

"More than once, at night, looking out of my window."

"You mean…like a ghost horse?"

"You're not going to laugh at me, are you?"

I crossed my heart.

"They say when someone is murdered, their spirit stays around until something is done about it. So why not a horse?"

"You think Centaur's spirit is hanging around to see justice done because his death wasn't an accident?"

"Maybe."

The stallion murdered? Was it possible that I had been visited by a ghost horse rather than by the real deal?

DAMIAN STOOD with his shoulder to the porch and watched Chloe with Nissa. He was impressed by the natural warmth she showed the girl—if only her mother had been half as attentive.

Nissa was finally healing. She'd come around with Dawn's attention, only to sink into another morass of depression and hostility with Dawn gone.

But this time Nissa bounced back quicker than the last. She was animated. Beaming. Sharing some secret with her tutor.

All Chloe's doing.

He'd thought Chloe Morgan a quiet thing when she'd first arrived, but she'd quickly disavowed him of that notion. She was soft. Softer than Dawn. Light-years softer than Priscilla. But she had a spine, as well, and she stood up for herself. Both were traits he appreciated.

Just as he appreciated the magic she'd worked on his daughter.

He wanted everything for Nissa. She was the one pure thing in his life. She had her whole life ahead of her, and she deserved all the good things that anyone could give her. Things he might not be able to give her now.

Fate could be a heartless bitch. It could take everything as easily as it gave. It could even take Nissa someday….

But he wouldn't think about that now.

Chloe and Nissa were nearly head-to-head. Suddenly they seemed so serious. Damian frowned.

There was a side to Chloe that still gave him pause. She was up to something. He didn't know what. She'd been wandering the house in the wee hours of the morning with a weak explanation. Did it have something to do with that damn horse? He needed to keep a closer eye on her. Now was as good a time as any to start.

He crossed to the gazebo. As if she sensed his gaze on the back of her neck, Chloe suddenly turned to him. Her pale gray eyes, the most prominent feature in her heart-shaped face, were opened wide, as if he had startled her.

He could get lost in those eyes....

Damian pulled himself together and looked past Chloe to Nissa, who seemed suddenly intent on her laptop.

Curious....

"How are you feeling?" he asked Chloe. "Any dizziness? Headache?"

"I'm fine. I thought you would know by now that Doc Haggerty gave me a clean bill of health."

"Just checking. You're not planning on riding today, are you? I don't have the time to go out with you."

While Chloe looked as if she wanted to say something tart in return, she agreed with him instead. "I thought I'd skip the riding today."

"Smart thinking."

"No one ever accused me of being dense."

He felt the rising tension between them when Nissa said, "Dad, stop picking on Chloe."

"I'm not picking on her."

"You're always telling her stuff that you don't have to, like she's a kid or something."

Wanting to smooth things over quickly, he inclined his head to Chloe. "Sorry if I offended you."

"You didn't." Chloe turned to Nissa. "Your dad is simply concerned."

"He's always concerned about *something,*" she said dramatically. "Usually about me."

"Now, Freckles, that's how fathers act with the daughters they love," Damian informed her.

"All fathers love their daughters."

"Some don't love their daughters nearly enough," Chloe returned. "But you don't have that problem."

A weird turn of conversation, making Damian wonder if Chloe had a problem with her own father. "So how is this morning's lesson going?"

"Nissa is proving to know more about horses than I knew there was to know." Chloe grinned at the tongue twister. "I said that right. Right?"

"Right." Damian found his lips lifting in return.

"Da-a-ad, you're interrupting. Chloe wants us to have a full tutoring session."

"Oh, excuse me. Just one more minute, I promise." He looked directly at Chloe when he said, "I won't be at lunch, so I need to ask this now."

"Ask what?"

"Nissa is going to a birthday party in Galena this evening, and—"

"You want me to take her?"

"Actually, I'm not trying to intrude on your personal time. Well, not exactly. I was going to take Chloe. But

I wondered if you would like to come into town and keep me company over dinner. Then, while I have a quick business meeting, you can browse through the stores. Most of them are open until eight or nine tonight. I'll catch up to you before it's time to pick up Nissa."

Chloe hesitated a heartbeat too long, and Damian figured he'd made a mistake in asking. "Sorry, I didn't mean to make you feel like I'm requiring you to do something you don't want to do."

Snapping out of her silence, Chloe said, "Actually, it sounds like a good plan. I would love to see more of Galena."

Damian noted how Nissa had pulled into herself, as if no one else were around. He hoped he hadn't done the wrong thing and set the girl off again. He also hoped his daughter didn't get the wrong idea about his asking Chloe to come to town with them. He wanted to get into the tutor's psyche—figure her out—nothing more personal than that.

Thinking he would find a moment to talk to his daughter alone and reassure her, Damian moved away, saying, "Break time's over."

"For all of us," Chloe said, turning her attention to Nissa.

And yet, Damian would bet she was aware of his every move as he headed back toward the barn.

Just as he was aware of her….

WHAT HAD GOTTEN into Damian to ask me to dinner? I wondered. Not wanting to get personally involved with anyone here—well, other than Nissa—I'd hesitated until I'd realized it was an opportunity to get more information out of my employer. If he would give it, that was.

Still, I couldn't help but look forward to a trip away from the horse farm. Not that I didn't like the place. The house was fascinating in its tawdry splendor, and the setting was magnificent. It was simply that I was a city girl, used to stepping out of my apartment and having myriad shops and forms of entertainment at my disposal, whereas here there were only horses.

My excitement had nothing to do with the fact that I'd be spending time alone with Damian.

Or so I tried to convince myself as I waited for Nissa to saddle Wild Cherry and lead her outside. She'd raced ahead of me into the barn. Since there was no adult to ride out with her, she was simply going to exercise her horse in one of the pastures, and I was going to watch.

In the meantime, I had the opportunity to mull over the bits I'd learned so far and to figure out a plan of attack for that evening.

I slipped my hand in my pocket and pulled out the hair clip. Holding it, looking at it, made me feel closer to my missing friend.

I closed my eyes and searched for Dawn in my mind. Her image was hazy, as if encased in fog. Just like the horse. How odd that the gray had led me straight to an object that belonged to my friend…assuming a real horse existed. At least I wasn't going crazy. Nissa had seen a gray, as well, though she believed the horse to be the ghost of Centaur, wandering through the mists searching for justice.

Too much for me to take in.

"I hear you're not riding."

Startled out of my thoughts, I nearly dropped the hair clip when I realized Clifford had come up on me without my being aware of him. "No, not today."

The groom stood a yard away from me, his narrow gaze dipping to my hand. Quickly I pocketed the hair clip, but not, I was certain, before he got a good look at it. If he recognized it as belonging to Dawn, however, he didn't say so.

"Was the mare not right for you, miss?"

"Sweet Innocent was wonderful. It's me. I tripped this morning, bumped my head."

"You're hurt?"

"No, really. I'm simply being overly cautious."

Clifford nodded. "Good thing. You get hurt around here and that's it for you."

Wondering what he meant by that, I asked, "Someone got hurt?"

"My brother used to work here, too," he told me. "Last year he had an accident. Messed up his leg. Don't work here no more."

"You mean he *can't* work? He's disabled?"

"He got a limp, but that ain't nothin'. Mr. Damian don't want him around no more. Hank can't support his family on disability. A man gives his all and when something happens—" Suddenly Clifford caught himself and made what looked like a concerted effort to calm down. "That's no nevermind of yours, though, miss."

"I'm sorry there's such trouble in your family." And that it troubled Clifford so deeply, making it sound as if he hated Damian.

But Clifford wasn't listening anymore. He was practically running away from me. Sensing someone behind me, I turned to see Theo Bosch standing there with his hands at his hips and wearing a disgusted expression.

"Sorry, miss," the barn manager said. "Clifford sometimes goes off at the mouth."

I shrugged. "I can only imagine how concerned he is about his brother."

"If he's so concerned, he should've done something about Hank's drinking problem before it got him into trouble."

"Oh."

"Now Clifford's lips are a little too loose sometimes. If that's all it is."

"I don't understand."

"Lots of stuff going wrong here, is all. It gets a man to wondering." He shook his head and, before I could comment, said, "There's Miss Nissa now."

I turned and waved, but Nissa's return wave before she mounted Wild Cherry was halfhearted at best. She'd been acting odd since this morning. No doubt she was feeling constrained having to keep to the pastures.

As I watched her work out her mare for the next hour, my mind kept drifting to the things I had learned, starting with the fact that Dawn's goodbye note was dated the day after she'd supposedly left and that I'd found her hair clip in an area she'd avoided like the plague, an area where a horse had fallen to his death…a horse that was—if one believed in ghosts—haunting the bluffs.

While Priscilla supposedly had left due to divorce, Nissa was convinced her mother was dead, and Theo had indicated Priscilla had simply disappeared, never to be seen again.

Mrs. Avery tried to keep me from learning anything about the family, plus she had subtly threatened me.

Damian was desperate to keep an ailing horse farm going, while Alex seemed desperate to get away from the business.

Bad luck had plagued the farm into near bankruptcy. And now Theo was suggesting Clifford might have had a hand in the misfortunes because of his brother.

Not a pretty picture.

Could any of this have something to do with Dawn's disappearance?

Chapter Eight

"You don't seem too excited about the party," I said. "Don't you want to go?"

Nissa shrugged.

"Anything I can do to help?"

"You already helped enough," she said, sounding put out.

"Young lady," Damian growled, "that's no way to talk to Chloe."

Ensconced in the front passenger seat of the black sedan—of course, Damian would drive a conservative car, I thought—Nissa sank into silence. And I finally figured out what was bothering her. "You" in the context of Damian and me, even if that wasn't true. He was merely being friendly inviting me to town and I was merely trying to take advantage of him. But in a thirteen-year-old's mind, I might represent a threat—a potential replacement for her mother.

I wondered if Mrs. Avery had anything to do with that. The housekeeper had stood on the front porch scowling after us. I'd felt very self-conscious. Theo and Clifford had been outside, as well. It seemed as if everyone on the property had been aware of us leaving together.

I only wished I could talk straight with Nissa and tell her that I wasn't in the running for a substitute of any kind in her personal life. But that, of course, was impossible.

"I hope you have a really good time tonight," I said. Nissa looked like a typical teen, in a ruffled miniskirt, embroidered jean jacket and boots. "You look so great, I'll bet you turn heads."

Damian said, "There are going to be *boys* at this party?"

"Da-a-ad!"

"And chaperones," I added.

Nissa had been complaining about her and her friends being treated like babies earlier.

Damian muttered something under his breath. All I got were the words "too fast." I smothered a smile. He was just being a normal, doting father.

Nissa should consider herself lucky.

Just after hitting town, we took a side road and climbed to a high spot dotted with old Victorian mansions on large lots. Damian stopped the car in front of one that I could only describe as steamboat Gothic in design, the ornate architectural style prevalent in the heyday of river travel. I'd read all about the Galena area before leaving Chicago.

Damian turned off the engine, undid his seat belt and started to open his door.

"Dad, you can't come with me!" Nissa protested. "They'll think I'm a baby."

Damian hardly missed a beat before saying, "I

wouldn't dream of coming with you. But I thought I could open the door for you since you're a young lady now." He glanced back at me. "And perhaps you would like to sit up front?"

In the end Damian opened both our doors, and Nissa and I ended up outside the car together.

"Don't forget your present," I said, reaching in and getting it for her. Then I lowered my voice. "You really do look spectacular."

Nissa couldn't help herself. She grinned at me and gave me a quick hug before grabbing the present and running for the stairs.

"They really do grow up too fast," I murmured, sliding into the passenger seat.

Damian sank into a thoughtful silence as we descended the hill and ended up on Main Street.

Even though it was early evening, families of tourists swarmed the sidewalks, going in and out of stores, eating ice cream and taffy and fudge. Everywhere kids were accompanied by parents. Those kids didn't even have a clue as to how lucky they were.

"I didn't think to ask you what kind of food you liked," Damian said.

"No real preferences," I said, bringing my thoughts back to him and the evening ahead. "We have just about anything you could ask for in Chicago, so I eat everything."

We settled on a charming little Italian place, which Damian claimed was a bit quieter than some of the others along Main Street. He parked the car in a lot near the Galena River a block behind the restaurant.

"I'm going to leave the car in the lot all evening," he

said as we walked to the restaurant. "I'll come back for it after my appointment and then pick you up. We'll figure out a place on Main Street."

"I can just meet you back here."

"You're sure? What if you beat me here? I don't have an extra set of keys on me."

"Then I'll wait for you. I'm a big-city girl, remember. I can handle it."

"I suppose it's safe enough."

That settled, we fell into a comfortable silence. But when we arrived at the restaurant, Damian guided me inside, his hand on my back. His light touch made me a little shaky. I took a deep breath and told myself he was simply being polite. Even so, I had to keep reminding myself that we weren't on a date—that he was my employer, a possible source of information about Dawn—especially when he helped me with my chair and leaned in so I could feel his warm breath stir the hair at my neck.

As he rounded the table to his seat, I took a quick look around—anywhere but at Damian—until I could compose myself. I certainly didn't want him to know he affected me. The interior of the restaurant was dark with sconces providing soft light at the walls, candles doing the same at each white-clothed, elegantly laid-out table. The romantic atmosphere played into that imagined-date thing.

"Can I get you something to drink?" the waitress asked, handing me a menu.

I looked at Damian.

"Wine?" he asked, and when I nodded, he told the waitress, "Two glasses of pinot grigio."

Indeed, it was quieter at this restaurant since customers were all adults. When I opened the menu, I knew why. Most people couldn't afford to feed a whole family at those prices. And Damian was having problems with money. So why had he brought me here?

Service was quick and helped me get my mind off the magnetic man across from me for a few moments. The waitress brought our glasses of wine and took our food orders.

Then Damian picked up his glass and toasted, "To Nissa's getting back to a normal life."

Warmed that his toast was to his child's welfare, I clinked glasses with him. "To Nissa."

Then Damian sat back in his chair, his gaze intent on me. "So what made you want to be a teacher?"

"Following in my mother's footsteps, I guess."

"She must be very proud of you."

"I hope she would be if she were here." No doubt my sadness showed; I suspected I would never get used to her being gone. "She died nearly a decade ago. Cancer."

"I'm sorry."

Damian placed a hand over mine in a gesture that was meant to be comforting, I was sure. Unease stirred in me at his touch instead, so I subtly removed my hand from under his by rearranging my shoulder bag near my feet. I wished I could still my racing pulse so easily.

"Your mother died when you were so young. I understand now why you have such a bond with my daughter."

"So Nissa's mother really *is* dead?"

Damian scowled. "Is she still telling people that fantasy? I simply meant Nissa's not having her mother in her life. Priscilla is very much alive."

"She is?" Could I believe him? Theo seemed to agree with Nissa. "Your daughter is convinced that her mother's gone for good."

"Simply because Priscilla hasn't been around."

"Damian, I know there's a certain awkwardness involved in a divorce..." My pulse started racing as I pushed the issue, both because I wanted Nissa to be happy and because I wanted to see what Damian would say about this proposal. "If that's the problem...I could help you work it out by taking Nissa to see her mother."

"No! There's nothing to be worked out. Priscilla may care about Nissa in her own way but evidently not enough to fight for her."

An answer that didn't sit well with me. "I was looking for a noncombative solution." When I got no response on that one, I added, "I don't understand why any woman wouldn't want to see her own daughter." Just as I hadn't understood why my father hadn't wanted to see me.

"It's best this way," Damian said coolly.

I shouldn't have been shocked at his attitude, but I was. Unless I was mistaken, *he* wanted it this way. "Keeping a child from a parent isn't right."

"You don't know the circumstances."

"Nothing justifies it."

"We'll have to agree to disagree, then."

I wanted to say more, to tell him how important it was for a girl that age to have both her parents, at least in some fashion, but what good would it do? My argument would only get Damian's back up and then what? He certainly wouldn't be receptive to me or any questions I might have.

And what if he'd lied about Priscilla being alive? a little voice whispered in my head.

I swallowed hard and fought not to think the worst. "You know best," I said, as if I'd conceded the point. "Maybe you should have a talk with Nissa about Priscilla, though, and try to convince the girl that her mother is alive."

"You think I haven't tried? Nissa is still a kid who believes in a world stocked with fairy-tale people. She has a very vivid imagination."

"Like her seeing the ghost horse?"

Damian glowered at me when he said, "You talked to her about that?"

"She talked to me. I simply listened. But I found it interesting that we've both seen this gray horse on the property, but you won't believe it."

"Twice I've been out looking for that damn horse after Nissa told me about it. You know what I've found? Nothing. Not even hoofprints in the earth."

I hadn't been able to find any physical trace of the horse, either, but I also knew what I had seen not once but twice. "Well, we're both having the same delusion, then."

Damian looked as if he had a headache. One named Chloe. I waited for him to chastise me again, but he'd closed up. Why would talking about the gray horse cause such a reaction from him? *Centaur.* That had to be it. He was connecting the dead horse with the one Nissa and I had seen. The girl insisted the gray was Centaur. Rather, his spirit.

Maybe we *had* seen a ghost horse….

The thought made me shiver.

Thankfully the waitress arrived with our food, breaking the tension. For a few minutes we ate in silence—Damian probably because he was angry with me, me because I was trying to figure out how to get information from the man without seeming too obvious.

"Nissa seems to be right on top of things," I began, hoping to distract him with a reason for parental pride. "Dawn did quite a good job with her. I wouldn't mind getting a look at her lesson plans. I was wondering if she left them behind."

"Mrs. Avery didn't find anything in her room—your room now. I suppose Dawn might have left school-related things in the library. That's where she worked with Nissa. Feel free to have a look."

Great. An excuse to be in the library and get at the computer without risking life and limb, and I thought I'd had no reason to do so again.

"Maybe I'll do that tomorrow," I said agreeably, paused, then said, "You know, Nissa really misses Dawn."

From the way he said, "I'm sure she does," I could tell that Damian wasn't a Dawn fan.

So what should I make of that? I wondered. As much as I loved Dawn and knew what a good person she was, she was also emotionally needy and sometimes put people off while trying to get their approval. Remembering she'd intimated the Graylord brothers were courting her, I wondered if she hadn't tried acting on that.

Undoubtedly, Damian would have been irritated if she'd made some kind of an advance toward him. Or…

again I wondered about Alex. If *he'd* done more than flirt with Dawn, that might have pushed *Damian's* hot button.

I couldn't stop myself from asking, "What did you think of Dawn?"

"No question that she's an excellent teacher. She developed a good rapport with my daughter."

"But not with the rest of the family? With you?"

"She wasn't to my taste, if that's what you're asking. But that's neither here nor there. She got Nissa back on the right road scholastically, and that's what concerned me."

"So you didn't like her?"

Damian set down his fork and narrowed his gaze on me. "What's all this interest in your predecessor?"

"Your daughter is emotionally vulnerable. She feels doubly abandoned. That's an additional challenge for me. I'm simply trying to do the best for her."

"I thought we already had this conversation."

Trying to hide my frustration was a challenge. I ate in silence for a few minutes before saying, "There's something you may not know about your daughter's emotional state…"

"But I'm sure you're going to tell me."

"She sleepwalks."

Damian put down his fork and narrowed his gaze on me. "What are you talking about? When?"

"I found her in my room the first night. She was okay, but she was looking for her mother while in her sleep. I got her back into her bed and tucked her in. She never woke up."

"This happened the night before last and you waited until *now* to tell me?"

"I meant to tell you earlier, but I didn't want to talk about the situation in front of Nissa. I was hoping to take you aside when we were out riding yesterday, but then the subject of the gray horse came up…and knocked the thought right out of me." I tried not to let my resentment at his disbelief in my story color my tone. "And I haven't exactly had the right opportunity since."

"Opportunity? When it comes to my daughter, I want you to make the opportunity. If there's a problem, I need to know about it immediately!"

"Yes, of course…. I'm so sorry, Damian."

Conversation didn't lull. It came to an abrupt halt. Great. Now Damian was angry with me. He was right, of course. I should have made it my business to tell him immediately. I'd let my own interests interfere. As much as I wanted to find out what had happened to Dawn, Nissa's welfare had to be my first concern.

So the dinner proved to be a bust.

Rather than getting answers, I was simply left with more questions.

GETTING AWAY FROM DAMIAN was a major relief. Walking down Main Street alone as the sun set, stopping in front of display windows of antique and other shops frequented by tourists, allowed me to breathe naturally again. At times I felt as if someone were watching me, but I put it to a combination of guilt and nerves. My employer was nowhere in the vicinity. I checked to make sure.

Damian Graylord was simply too much for me to handle, and as I entered an antique shop, I wondered what had made me think that I could play detective and figure out what had happened to my friend. I should have hired a private investigator. Not that I had the money to do so.

Besides, there was no one who cared more about Dawn than I did—except, perhaps, this supposed new husband whom no one had met.

Inside the store, I looked around at furniture and collectables from the Victorian era and forward. Dawn and I loved to rummage through stores like this in hopes of making a find we could afford to bring home. We had done so before she'd taken the job schooling Nissa.

If only her position at her school hadn't been cut, she wouldn't have been day-to-day subbing, wouldn't have taken the temporary position away from home, wouldn't be missing now with no one but me to care. And Nissa. If the girl knew Dawn really hadn't run off on her, she would be even more upset than she already was.

Hoping to find something to take me out of this mood, I looked around more carefully until my gaze lit on an object that stuck out like a sore thumb.

The horse was a miniature of one of those life-size ponies painted by artists out west a couple of years before. This one's side was decorated with four Thoroughbred horses charging down the home stretch, the leader a nose ahead of the others. The silks of the jockeys were in bright contrast to the midnight-black background.

The find delighted me. Thinking that Nissa would love it, I thought to buy it for her.

But as I reached for it, my hand collided with another.

"Sorry," we both said at once.

The other interested party was a good-looking man with light brown hair and dark brown eyes. He seemed familiar somehow, but I couldn't place him.

"Go ahead," the man urged. "If you really want the horse, please, it's yours. My niece probably has too many of these things, anyway."

"Are you sure? We both reached for it at the same time. We could flip a coin."

"I wouldn't want to stop you from buying a souvenir to take home."

"Oh, I'm not a tourist. I don't mean I'm a local, but I'm working here for the summer. The girl I'm tutoring is crazy about horses."

"Really?" he said, his inflection indicating interest. "Well, I *insist* you take it."

"I feel kind of bad…"

"Then stroll with me for a little while if you want me to feel better. There's a great antique store down the street that you would probably love."

"I don't know."

"You can help me pick out a gift for my niece."

He was being so generous and charming, and I was feeling a little guilty that I really wanted that horse for Nissa. I didn't know how to put him off nicely. I checked my watch and said, "I really have to meet my employer at the parking lot by the river in a half hour."

"Plenty of time to check out just one more shop. The name's Jack."

"Chloe."

His being so nice trapped me into saying yes. So after I paid for the horse, I left with him and headed for another shop filled with collectibles. Jack was attractive and had a winning smile, so why did I feel so weird accompanying him? We were only browsing, for heaven's sake.

As we strolled down the street, storefronts and streetlamps now lit brightly against the dark, he asked, "So how do you like Galena?"

"It's lovely. This is my first time in town."

"So you're staying someplace in the country?"

"A horse farm."

"Not Graylord Pastures?" He asked this so quickly that I thought he must have somehow already known it.

"That's it."

He stopped in the street, the shop seemingly forgotten. "So, you're the teacher they brought in to replace the one who left last month."

"You know the Graylords?"

"Very well, actually."

That put me on alert. I wondered what he knew that I should. And I wondered how to get any pertinent information out of him.

"Where is that store you wanted me to see?" I asked.

"Oh, sorry. Right here." He indicated the next store and let me lead the way inside before asking, "So where do you hail from? Dubuque? Rockford?"

"Chicago."

His eyebrows raised fractionally. "Really. The other girl was from Chicago, as well."

Wondering how he'd known that, I shrugged and moved past him to a chest of drawers set out with old jewelry. No doubt gossip about outsiders was rife in a small area like this. Hopefully, that would make him inclined to do likewise.

"Dawn and I were listed with the same agency."

"So you knew her."

"Chicago is a huge city," I murmured, pretending I was interested in a pair of rhinestone earrings from the fifties. "I couldn't possibly know everyone in the system. There are thousands of teachers."

"You called her Dawn, so it sounded like you knew her."

Not wanting to lie outright, I continued to hedge. "Nissa talks about Dawn. They were quite fond of each other. Did you know her?"

His gaze on me felt intense, as if he was trying to read me. Why…I didn't know. His dark brown eyes seemed shuttered, as if he were keeping me at a distance. Could he tell I was dabbling in half-truths?

"I met her," he finally said. "Nice girl."

"Odd how she up and married some guy she'd just met."

"Very odd. What do you think about this?" he asked, holding up a teddy bear.

"How old is your niece?"

"Um…fifteen."

I shook my head. "So, did you ever see Dawn with this new husband of hers?"

"Afraid not." Jack grabbed a tiny bag seeded with pearls. "What about this?"

"That's more like it."

"Hmm, let me think about it." He returned the bag to its table.

"So where did you meet her?" Somehow I didn't think it was at the farm.

"The first time? I don't recall. We ended up at a few of the same social events here in town."

"Maybe you saw her with the very man she married."

"If I did, I don't remember."

Disappointed that either he wasn't being forthcoming or he didn't know more, I moved on to a display of old photographs in equally old frames and quickly changed the subject to another that interested me.

"I suppose you knew Priscilla, too," I said, watching for his reaction.

"I had her number, yes."

A weird thing to say, but not out of line with everything I'd been hearing. And his expression was neutral, so it didn't seem he had anything personal against the ex-Mrs. Graylord.

"I'm just a little worried about Nissa. She so wants to see her mother."

"That might be difficult, considering the circumstances."

"Priscilla lives in town, right?"

"Where did you get that idea?"

"I just assumed—"

"Wrong," Jack finished for me. "Priscilla Graylord did a disappearing act. God only knows what happened to her. God and maybe Damian Graylord."

There it was again, that intimation of foul play. "That certainly sounds ominous."

"For all we know, Damian locked her away in the attic and threw away the key. He and Priscilla didn't get along."

The attic reference got to me. All those noises I'd been hearing above me…Mrs. Avery warning me the attic was off-limits…her stopping me when I tried…

I shook away the fanciful thoughts and said, "Obviously, they had some serious problems. That's why they're divorced."

"They didn't get along for *years.* I'm sure the final straw was Priscilla running the farm's finances into the ground. The only question I have is…what took Damian so long to get rid of her?"

The breath caught in my throat at the last part of Jack's statement…"get rid of her." Did he really mean it the way it sounded?

"I'm sure he tried to work out his marriage for Nissa's sake."

"Yeah, he dotes on the kid. He's determined to keep Graylord Pastures intact for her. Considering the way his empire has been crumbling, he's a little delusional."

"What would you have him do?"

"Tighten his belt. Sell some of the hoof stock, part of the property."

Now I knew why Jack had seemed familiar. He was the neighbor Damian had been arguing with—Jack Larson. He'd also been after Dawn, or so she'd told Nissa. And he was acting as if he barely knew her.

Not that I was going to let on I was aware of any of this.

"I'm sure Damian will do whatever it takes to hang on as long as possible." Maybe he could even find those diamonds Alex had told me about. "His losing Graylord Pastures is unthinkable."

"Sometimes the unthinkable happens."

I was really not liking Jack Larson. "Well, we can hope not."

"Right. So has anything new happened at the farm?"

"New?"

"Any new bad luck? I haven't heard about any more catastrophes since he lost that stallion."

"I wouldn't know."

"No more equipment breakdowns or fires?"

"Not that I've heard," I said, my voice tightening.

I suspected Jack Larson had known who I was when I'd walked into that first antique shop. He could have seen me coming out of the restaurant with Damian and followed me to get information about the farm from me. Information he could use to squeeze Damian?

The idea gave me the creeps.

I said, "Listen, it's been enlightening, but I need to get going."

"What a shame. We were just getting to know each other. What are you doing tomorrow night?" he asked smoothly.

"I'm afraid I'll be busy."

"The night after?"

"Busy."

"The night after that?" His lips curled. "I suppose you'll be busy then, too."

"I suppose I will." I was already backing away. "Good luck finding something."

"What?"

His instant confusion convinced me he hadn't been looking for a present for any niece but had been using the excuse to talk to me.

"For your niece," I reminded him, before whipping away and hotfooting it out of the store.

I stood outside for a moment to get my bearings. It was dark now and everything looked different. Glancing down the street, I spotted the store where Jack had intercepted me. Beyond that, on the other side of the street, would be the restaurant, and a block behind that, the parked car.

Figuring out my directions to the parking lot, I crossed the street and felt a tingle down my spine. I glanced back. Jack stood outside the store, staring after me. I hurried and—though the parking lot was still a block or so farther along—turned down a side street just so I didn't have to feel Jack's gaze on the back of my neck.

What a position I'd put myself in. First I'd agreed to have dinner with Damian in hopes of getting him to open up. Not only had I put him off in several different ways, but then I'd left myself open to be a target of his business rival. I hoped Damian never heard about it.

Few people ventured away from the Main Street shops. The sidewalks were pretty much deserted, and only a few cars circled, their drivers undoubtedly searching for parking. Though streetlights were on, they barely cut through the dark, the spooky atmosphere filling me with a growing sense of unease. I turned again and the way was laden with shadows. The street seemed my safest bet. In Chicago if I came home late at night, I walked down the middle of the street. So I quickly hurried into the open, away from the dark corners, breathing easier only when I saw the parking lot ahead.

My relief didn't last long.

The thrum of an engine behind me had me glancing over my shoulder into the brights of a dark car creeping along behind me. I moved to the side of the street to let the vehicle pass, but it stayed equidistant from me.

I hurried faster.

Just as I got in the open to cross to the other side of the street, a squeal of tires screeched up my spine, and I whirled around.

The now-speeding vehicle jumped out of the dark toward me.

Chapter Nine

"Stop!" I shouted, blinded by the brights and trying to move feet that felt rooted to the ground.

The next seconds unraveled in slow motion:

...forcing a foot to step toward the sidewalk...

...the brights looming closer...

...fumbling with the package that escaped my grasp...

...stepping out of the path of the speeding car even as I felt its metal breath...

And then I tripped on the curb and went sprawling.

"Hey, are you all right?" a male voice called.

I blinked and saw a couple running toward me. Strangers. I couldn't get a breath to answer.

"Call for an ambulance," the woman said.

The man pulled out his cell phone, but I choked out, "No...not hit."

"Are you sure?"

"I tripped, but I'm okay." Bruised from the fall, probably, but not otherwise hurt.

"Let me help you up."

I took the hand the man offered and let him pull me

to my feet. He was an older man with a weathered face and receding hairline, but he was still strong.

His companion, in good physical shape, also, stooped over in the street, saying, "Too bad I didn't see the guy's license plate or I'd get the cops after him."

"Too bad," I echoed.

Her voice apologetic, the woman offered me the object she'd picked up—a crumpled bag. "I think he ran over this."

I nodded and looked inside at the smashed horse and thought that could have been me. The back of my throat felt tight and my eyes felt hot. I blinked back tears and fought the undoubtedly normal reaction.

"Reckless driver," the woman said, shaking her head.

Reckless? I didn't think so. I was certain whoever had been behind the wheel had meant to hit me. But why? I had no enemies…unless, of course, someone knew why I was here and had reason to hide the truth of Dawn's disappearance.

Did that mean I was getting close?

Jack Larson had avoided my question about Dawn….

I realized the man and woman were staring at me with concern.

"I really am all right," I assured them. "But thank you both for your help."

"You seem to be in shock," the man said. "You shouldn't be alone. We can see you home."

"No, the car is here."

"Then we'll walk you to it…but are you sure you're in any condition to drive?"

I was already scanning the lot for Damian's dark

sedan, but the vehicle eluded me. I frowned. "It's not here." We'd parked near the street, but the car was gone.

"You mean someone stole your car?"

"Not mine."

Where in the world had he gone?

Before I could explain, a vehicle pulled up along the curb and Damian alighted, saying, "Chloe, sorry I'm late."

"Oh, your husband is here," the woman said, sounding relieved. "Good."

"We'll just get going, then." To Damian the man said, "Your wife is a lucky woman."

"Thank you both," I said again, as the couple headed off across the lot.

"Husband?" Damian asked, sounding piqued. "What's going on?"

"Their assumption," I assured him. "They helped me after a car almost hit me."

His expression changed instantly. "Are you hurt? Should you be on your feet? Let me help you into the car, for God's sake."

"I'm fine," I protested, though I didn't fight him when he put an arm across my back to help me to the car. "The horse isn't."

"Horse?"

I held out the bag. "I bought it for Nissa. B-but I can't give it to her n-now." My voice caught in a sob as the reality of what had almost happened to me hit home.

"You're trembling."

Damian drew me against his chest and held me lightly while I tried to pull myself together. My emotions spun out of control, and for a moment I clung to him as if he were my lifeline.

"Thank goodness you're all right," he murmured, his hand stroking the length of my spine.

As Damian soothed me, my nerves steadied, if not the trembling, which now had a very different source. My knees felt weak and my pulse felt strong. My heart was beating so rapidly I could feel its constant thump. Could he? Did he know how attracted I was to him?

His hand distracted me from the near collision. Each of his long fingers left a trail of exquisite sensation rippling along my spine. The ripples spread outward as if in concentric circles until my entire body was enveloped by his energy. I wasn't the only one affected. His features went taut, his gaze narrowing on my face, my mouth.

"I'm sorry I wasn't here," he murmured, making me wonder where he had been.

My lips parted and my tongue darted out, an indication of my sudden nerves. Then his mouth closed over mine, and he stole away what breath I had left. My mind left me, and all that was left was sensation. The inviting wet warmth of his mouth…the scintillating sharpness of his teeth…the turgid thrust of his tongue.

I tried losing myself in that kiss, but in my mind I once again saw the brightness of those lights coming at me, and I jerked away from him and stepped back.

We stood inches apart, breathing hard. For a moment I saw something in his expression that surprised me. But before I could define it, the moment was over.

"I apologize," he murmured.

"No need."

"I took advantage—"

"We shared a moment, that's all. Now it's over!" I said sharply.

Damian pulled back as if I'd struck him. I almost apologized…but I didn't. Too many unanswered questions lay between us. Now there was another. He'd told me he meant to leave the car in the lot, but he'd changed his mind. Why? I refused to draw conclusions, but the car that had come at me had been a dark sedan….

I didn't want to believe Damian was so duplicitous that he tried to run me over one minute and then kissed me the next. But how could I be sure?

I shook my head. First I'd considered Jack Larson to be the culprit…now Damian. I wasn't thinking clearly at all. That much was obvious.

"Nissa is waiting," I said.

"What about this?" He held up the bag.

I indicated a nearby trash can. "I don't want Nissa to see it. She'll want to know what happened."

Damian nodded and threw the bag in the wire container. By the time he got back to the car, I was already in the passenger seat.

"We should stop at the police station on the way home."

"Why?"

"To make out a report."

"Which would make sense if I could actually describe the car or the driver. Or if I was hurt, which I'm not."

"Well, I'm going to call it in. Probably the driver was drunk."

I didn't want to protest too much lest Damian's suspicions were aroused. So I sat frozen while he placed the call on his cell. I was too freaked to listen to what he was saying. I only hoped this call wouldn't be my undoing, that I wouldn't be found out and sent packing.

"Okay, thanks, Sam," Damian said, then snapped his cell closed. "He's going to send a patrol car around looking for the reckless driver."

I breathed a sigh of relief as we started off.

It only took a few minutes to get to the house on the hill, but enough time for me to play that near miss over and over in my mind a dozen times.

When Damian left the car to fetch Nissa, I watched him walk to the house, wondering if he was simply what he seemed to be—a concerned father, a hardworking horseman, a decent human being…or something far darker.

Damian had come to my rescue twice now, and both times he could have been responsible.

That morning I'd tried to believe I'd imagined hands at my back, but now it seemed certain they'd been as real as the speeding car. Someone had shoved me. Someone had tried to run me over. The *same* someone?

Were both incidents merely warnings?

Or had someone really meant to kill me?

Surely Jack Larson hadn't been inside the Graylord house at dawn. Who then did that leave?

Damian Graylord?

If so, then what might he have done to Dawn?

"YOU HAVE TO COME into my room to talk," Nissa whispered as we entered the house.

I couldn't ignore Nissa's hopeful, excited expression. I was certain that this was an evening on which she would be well served to have her mother to talk to…but all she had was me in the way of another female. I looked back to see if Damian had noticed Nissa's exhilaration, but he hadn't followed us into the house. I looked through the open doorway and saw him walking off toward the barns.

"All right," I said, closing the door. "I'll be there in a few minutes."

I wanted to clean up first, make certain there were no telltale signs of my hitting the pavement. I didn't want Nissa questioning me. No need to upset her further.

Nissa had been calm and collected in the car when answering her father's myriad questions about the party. I hadn't known if he normally would have been so interested or if it had been his way of avoiding me, but either way I'd been relieved to have time to collect myself.

That time obviously was at an end.

It only took a few minutes to change into jeans and a T-shirt. It took a few more for me to steady myself when all I could think about was Damian and that kiss. I glanced out the window. The yard outside the barn was lit but, try as I might, I couldn't spot Damian or anyone else.

Not wanting to stall any longer, I closed my mind against what had happened between us earlier and went to Nissa's room. The door was open a crack. Nissa was humming to herself. I smiled and knocked. The next moment, Nissa was grabbing my hand and dragging me inside.

"Whoa," I said, laughing. "You must have had a good time tonight."

"The best." Looking as if she were about to burst, Nissa closed her door and moved away from it. "There's this boy..."

"Ah, one of those."

"His name is Kyle Warren and he's really cute. You won't tell Dad, right?"

"That all depends on what exactly you and Kyle did."

Nissa seemed puzzled for a second. And then horror-struck. "Not tha-a-at."

"What, then?"

Relieved, I listened attentively as she told me about her evening. How Kyle had told her he was glad to see her again. How he said he was happy she was coming back to school. How they danced together. Twice. I commented in all the right places and drew her out further. A happy Nissa was a more attractive Nissa. Tonight she was blooming before my eyes.

Then she grimaced as if she were steeling herself. "Kyle, um, well, he kissed me..." she said in not much more than a whisper.

"O-o-oh. Your first kiss?"

"With Kyle. Sammy Crane kissed me in the third grade, but that doesn't count 'cause it was kid stuff. It lasted like maybe one second."

Ironically Nissa and I both had been kissed tonight. And from the way I'd felt in Damian's arms, everything before him had been kid stuff, too.

"This kiss lasted longer," she went on. "I almost counted to five. I just don't know if I did it right." Sighing, she plopped down next to me on the bed.

Uh-oh, this conversation could quickly become questionable territory. I didn't want anything I said to come back to bite me later. Heaven forbid I get into something with her that Damian wouldn't like. Yet, I couldn't simply abandon her.

"Kissing comes naturally, Nissa. I'm sure you did just fine." I didn't want to know the details. "But that's all you did, right? Just kiss?"

"I told you that was all."

"Because boys your age can be very precocious."

"I'm precocious, too. Dad gave me the birds-and-bees talk, okay? I'm not into all that."

"Good. You're too young."

Now I was doubly uncomfortable. Counseling Nissa on sex wasn't part of my job description, and I didn't think Damian would appreciate my taking on the task. I didn't have enough experience to be an expert in the subject, anyway. Thankfully, I quickly realized Nissa really *wasn't* into all that. She'd simply wanted someone she could tell about her exciting evening—her first real kiss—and I was touched that she'd turned to me.

"Chloe, how do you know when a guy really likes you?"

I thought about it for a moment. "I guess there's something about the way he looks at you."

Like the way Damian looked at me....

"Kyle's got the coolest blue eyes. They go all squinty when he talks to me."

"Well, then..."

"He tried to carry my books once last fall."

Hmm, sounded like a long-term crush on Kyle's part. "Did you let him?"

"I punched him and told him I could do it myself. Was that wrong?"

I bit the inside of my lip so I wouldn't laugh. Nissa might be thirteen, but I was getting the picture she was a very young thirteen—at least in comparison to sexually wiser city girls—when it came to boys.

"Perhaps you weren't ready to let Kyle carry your books. Maybe you won't ever want him to, but maybe next time you'll tell him no and thank him rather than punch him."

"Next time I think I'll let him."

We grinned at each other in understanding.

"You really are cool, Chloe. The only other person I could talk to like this was Dawn."

"She gave you good advice?"

"She told me to know my own mind, to figure out what I wanted out of life and to go after it."

That sounded exactly like Dawn.

"I guess that's why she eloped," Nissa went on. "I just wish I could still see her sometimes."

"Me, too, honey."

Nissa gave me a curious expression. "But you didn't know her."

Quickly, I covered. "I meant I wished that *for you.*"

"Oh."

Figuring this was my cue to leave, I got to my feet, saying, "It's getting late. Nearly eleven." And despite her excitement, Nissa seemed to be suppressing a yawn. "Time to get ready for bed."

"Okay." She gave me a quick hug. "Night."

I hugged her in return and headed for the door, trying not to show how stiff my aching muscles felt. "Sweet dreams."

Undoubtedly her dreams would be sweet tonight. I wasn't so sure about my own. I had a lot on my mind, starting with the car incident.

I took a long, hot shower to soothe my aching body. Two falls in one day had left me sore and bruised. But at the same time, I couldn't put Damian and that kiss we'd shared out of my mind. I might have been thinking of him as a suspect, but I desired him, as well.

The needles of water pinging against my back made me think of his hand running up my spine. The sensation was nearly the same. I turned, and the water hit my breasts. My nipples tightened into hard points. My flesh betrayed me and, letting my eye flutter closed, I imagined for a moment what it might be like to be joined with Damian here in the shower. On the bed. Anywhere....

I tried to shake myself free of the disturbing sensations, to no avail. They followed me out of the shower and into my bed. Thinking about the attacks on me, I chose to leave the bedside lamp burning low. If someone made it past my locked door, I at least wanted to be able to see the threat. Outside my windows, the sky was dark. I stared out into the night as if it could give me answers.

Tomorrow, I thought. I needed sleep. I needed a clear head. But sleep wouldn't come. I tossed and turned for what seemed like hours; though, according to the bedside clock, mere minutes passed.

Using meditation techniques, I relaxed my body...relaxed my mind...took myself to another place....

I walk through the dark on a path I've traveled before. It feels familiar, yet not. Trees loom over me like giants, leaves rustling, whispering warnings.

"Go back, go back!"

"Someone knows…"

"You'll never escape alive."

Fear drives me. Not fear for myself, but fear that I'll never find the truth, never find Dawn.

"Ci-Ci," the wind whispers.

Only Dawn calls me Ci-Ci. I think I hear her voice through the trees. I run faster. Searching. Always searching. Never really finding.

"Dawn, where are you? I need to know."

"I'm here. Go back."

"Where? Why?"

Danger….

The word whistles through me, leaving a trail of raised flesh along my spine. I turn and turn and look for the danger but see nothing. Finally I gasp, out of breath, and stop just for a moment.

That's when the fog parts and he steps out of the mists.

Damian….

THE WATCHER STOOD opposite the house, opposite her room, gaze glued to her lit bedroom windows. Willing her to leave was doing no good. It was obvious she wouldn't go. She had nine lives, that one, with seven left.

Not that the attempts had been meant to kill her…not yet. They'd been meant to scare her into going. The watcher didn't want to kill anyone.

Not even that damn horse.

Ghost horse…the words seemed to whisper through the air…that's what she'd been telling people.

Not that it was believable. Not any more than Chloe Morgan being exactly what she said she was. Oh, she might be a teacher, all right, but she had her own agenda for being here, one that had to do with Dawn Reed.

But why? What was the connection?

If only she would just go away. Stop poking her nose where it didn't belong. If she didn't, there would be no choice.

Don't make me kill you….

Chapter Ten

I was hearing noises again, though this time not from the attic. As I waited for Nissa to come from her room to have breakfast with me, I stopped in front of the dining room fireplace and listened. The sounds seemed to be whispering downward from the other side of the wall.

Stairs? Surely not.

My pulse drummed hard. Too many weird things went on, both in and out of this house. Too many involving me. I felt the need to solve some mystery—even a small one—so that I could justify my very presence at Graylord Pastures.

More sounds, closer now….

The noise couldn't be coming from the back staircase accessible through the kitchen. They were too far away. Since there was a door leading out of the dining room to the back of the house, I opened it to see. Nope. No stairs. And now no noise, either.

So what had I heard?

I studied what appeared to be a mudroom behind the parlor. Barn coats hung from hooks, and calf-high rubber boots and shoes lined up neatly along a rubber tray. The room had three other doors. I checked each of them. One led to the outside, another to a butler's pantry, a third to a storage area filled with cleaning tools and household staples from boxed food to paper goods.

No stairs.

How peculiar.

As I headed back to the dining room, something odd struck me. The wall to my left seemed longer than that of the storage room. I went back to check by pacing off the length from the inside, then pacing off the length on the mudroom side. Sure enough, there was a three-foot or so difference.

Returning to the dining room, I carefully studied the wall. Was there a hollow behind it that had something to do with the way the fireplace had been built? I wondered. They seemed to be equally deep.

Curious now, I crossed the hall to the library and that fireplace. Indeed it seemed as if the wall in the hallway leading to the vestibule contained empty space…almost as if the house had secret passages.

"Can I help you with something, miss?"

Nearly jumping out of my skin, I turned to meet Mrs. Avery's disapproval with a shaky smile.

"No, thank you. I was just passing time waiting for Nissa to get herself downstairs for breakfast."

As if on cue, footsteps clunked down the nearby staircase. I noted how different, how immediate, this sounded compared to what I'd heard a few minutes before. Totally different from the muffled sounds in the dining room.

Focusing on Mrs. Avery, I said, "There she is now."

"Which has nothing to do with your being in the library," the housekeeper said, her expression sour.

I couldn't help myself. I was tired of being browbeaten when I'd done nothing wrong. "Before you tell me the library is off-limits, Damian has said otherwise."

Mrs. Avery sniffed and walked straight-spined to the kitchen. And I couldn't help but smile at my small victory as I watched her go.

"Morning, Chloe," Nissa said, grinning when she saw me.

The girl's smile warmed me inside and made me put out of mind the old harridan of a housekeeper.

What I couldn't forget were the mysterious noises bothering me with increasing frequency. There was so much going on that I couldn't explain. Noises...horses that didn't exist...hands that shoved and cars that threatened....

So after eating, as we strolled to the gazebo for our morning session—even though it was Saturday, we were going to work for a few hours—I casually asked, "How many staircases does the house have?"

"Just the main one and the one off the kitchen. Why?"

"Oh, my imagination is sparked, I guess. You hear all about hidden staircases having been built into some of these big old houses as a way for servants to take shortcuts."

Nissa shrugged. "I know there were supposedly tunnels and secret passageways—Dad and Uncle Alex got stuck in one when they were kids. Then Granddad had them sealed off."

"Tunnels and secret passages?" My pulse ticked at the thought. "But you don't know where?"

"Nope. I tried to find my way into one when I was a kid, but I never did. I figured maybe Dad and Uncle Alex were just teasing me."

When she was a kid…as if she was so grown-up now.

Suddenly sensing we weren't alone, I glanced over my shoulder to see Theo standing stock-still and staring after us. I hadn't even realized the barn manager was there. He must have heard our entire conversation. Not that it should account for his strange expression.

"Morning," I said.

"Morning, miss."

I felt his gaze on the back of my neck as we entered the gazebo and settled in. I glanced back the way we'd come, but Theo was gone. What was his deal? I wondered, then thought how awful it felt to be suspicious of everything and everyone. Self-preservation in a new form.

"So, what should I work on today?" Nissa asked, snapping me back to the moment.

"What would you like to work on?"

"Me? I get to choose?"

"Being Saturday…today you do."

"I can choose anything?"

"As long as it has some direct learning value." When she gave me a blank stare, I prompted her, "As in English, math, geography, history—"

"History! The history of horse racing in America."

I laughed. "History it is."

For a while, I lost myself with Nissa. But eventually darker circumstances invaded my thoughts.

Secrets…disappearances…danger…

Jack Larson telling me Priscilla might be locked up in the attic. Intimating worse.

Someone trying to run me over…

"Chloe, is something wrong?"

I blinked and saw that Nissa was frowning in concern. "Oh, my mind was just wandering," I said, hedging. The truth, if not the details. "I'm fine." At least for the moment.

"You looked like I feel sometimes."

Her voice trembled and I knew she was having a bad moment and it was all my fault. I reached out for her and gave her a hug and maybe held on to her a bit longer than I might have if all these strange things hadn't been happening to me. Nissa clung to me, and I felt as if she would never let me go.

Part of me yearned for this—this feeling of belonging. I'd had it with my mother and I'd had it with Dawn. I feared to get too close to Nissa, though.

How would my leaving affect her?

How would it affect me?

I dreaded finding out.

APPROACHING THE GAZEBO to see if Nissa and Chloe wanted to ride before lunch, Damian stopped within yards of the structure when the tutor put her arms around his daughter. Nissa's response was instant and totally natural—she hugged Chloe in return.

Watching them together, his chest tightened. For a moment Nissa looked the way he always wanted to see her—truly happy. She'd rarely worn that look of pure, positive emotion in her short lifetime. Sometimes she had with him. Never with her own mother. With Priscilla, Nissa had always seemed more hopeful than fulfilled, as if she knew from toddlerhood that her mother only had so much to give her.

The girl had craved more—that had always been obvious. He'd seen the longing written on Nissa's face when she was with Priscilla too many heart-wrenching times to count. No wonder she preferred to think her mother was dead. Better than admitting that she'd been abandoned by the parent who was supposed to love her.

Damian swallowed the guilt the last triggered in him. He was responsible, but he'd done what he'd had to—he'd been protecting his child. And it wasn't as though Priscilla hadn't asked for it, after all. She was a selfish bitch who'd always loved herself best.

Not Chloe, though. The tutor was full of surprises.

As if she were privy to his thoughts, Chloe looked his way and immediately let go of Nissa and straightened in her chair, seeming…embarrassed? Then his daughter realized he was there.

"Dad!" she called, waving, her freckled face made prettier by a dazzling smile.

Grinning in return, Damian moved forward and stopped at the entrance to the gazebo. "Could you stand to be interrupted this morning?" he asked Chloe directly.

"That all depends on the nature of the interruption."

Did she think he wanted to chide her for some new transgression? Remembering their disagreement over dinner the night before, Damian figured she might hold that in the realm of possibilities.

"All depends on whether or not you're ready for another horseback ride. It would have to be this morning, though, since Alex and Nissa and I are going to a friend's house for a get-together and dinner late this afternoon."

"You'll take us?" Nissa asked excitedly. "Yay!"

"There's one vote for it." Damian arched an eyebrow at Chloe. "What say you?"

"Sounds great!"

"Get yourselves together, then, ladies, and I'll have Clifford ready your horses. Meet me at the barn in fifteen minutes?"

Chloe was already gathering her things. "We'll have to hurry if you want to change, Nissa."

"I'm hurrying!" Nissa said as Damian set off for the barns. "Riding horses is even better than researching them. I'm psyched."

Damian didn't miss the excited laughter behind him. He glanced over his shoulder. Both of them seemed so happy, he had to smile himself.

Chloe had certainly changed the atmosphere around Nissa. Dawn had been good in her own way. But she'd also been emotionally needy, her demand for attention nearly as sharp as his daughter's. That *hadn't* been good for Nissa, who needed someone sure enough of herself to be a steady influence. Nissa needed a Chloe in her life.

As do you...a little voice whispered.

Not that it would do him any good. Chloe Morgan was young. She was a city girl. She had certain standards. Expectations. No matter that the attraction between them was growing. No matter that they'd shared that kiss.

A mistake.

Damian had known that even as he'd held her in his arms.

If the lovely tutor knew what he'd done to protect Nissa...the farm...their very way of life...Chloe Morgan would run from him as fast as she could.

Not that there was any need for her to know anything he didn't care to tell her. She was here for the summer, no more. He couldn't let it be more. However, he could enjoy her company, enjoy watching her with Nissa, while subduing his deeper desires.

With that settled, he found Clifford and asked the groom to tack up Sweet Innocence and Wild Cherry, while he saw to Sarge himself.

Twenty minutes later they were riding out toward the palisades. He let Nissa take the lead and was content to ride alongside Chloe.

"The family will be leaving for that get-together about four. I've given the staff the night off, so I'm afraid you'll have to see to your own dinner. If you want to go into town, I'd be happy to buy."

"Actually, I could use some downtime. If I have permission to rummage through the refrigerator, I won't starve."

"Permission granted. You're sure?"

"I look forward to spending a few hours on my own. I could use a few hours alone."

Or maybe she wanted to avoid Galena after almost being run over. "No ill effects from last night?" he asked.

"A few sore spots. Bruises."

"You were lucky."

She didn't say anything. He wondered if she was thinking about the car coming at her or if she was thinking about the kiss that followed.

He figured she might comment on one or the other, so he was surprised when she said, "Tell me about the secret passageways in the house."

"How do you know about them?"

"Nissa."

Damian chuckled. "That girl never forgets anything."

"Actually, since she never could find them, she wasn't sure if you were telling her the truth or having a laugh at her expense."

"There was nothing funny about getting trapped in the dark, believe me," Damian assured her. "I was twelve and Alex was ten. We'd only just discovered them and started exploring the system that ran through parts of the house when Alex found a doorway to an underground tunnel. I told him not to go in there, but he wouldn't listen. He wanted to see where it led."

"So you went in after him?"

"That's what big brothers are for."

"To get into mischief with their siblings."

Damian laughed, remembering. "We got into trouble, all right. The door jammed closed so we had to walk the entire length of the tunnel to look for an exit, and a few minutes in, the flashlight batteries went."

"Then what happened?"

"We felt our way out to the palisades, but that exit was blocked by rock. We could see out to the river, but the openings weren't big enough to squeeze through.

Trust me, Alex tried his best, and he was pretty scrawny at the time."

Thinking she might be amused by the story, he glanced at Chloe and wondered at her thoughtful expression.

"So how *did* you get out?" she asked.

"When we didn't show up for dinner, the whole household searched for us. Luckily, we didn't secure the secret door we used to get into the passageways, so Dad figured it out and got the tunnel door open. I was never so glad to hear his voice, even though he was angry."

"I assume there were consequences."

"We went to bed hungry, but Dad decided the lesson was enough punishment."

"Nissa said he had the passageways sealed up."

"He figured the lure was too much for two nosy boys to resist. He was right."

"So you're sure he sealed all the entrances?"

Again the serious expression, Damian noted. "Trust me. Alex and I checked it out. To our great disappointment, we were locked out. Why are you so interested?"

"Our childhoods tell us a lot about who we are."

"What does this story tell you?"

"That you thought you were in charge even then. And while Alex isn't exactly a leader, he isn't a follower, either. He goes his own way, no matter the consequences."

"Wow, you got all that from one story?"

"The story…and personal observation."

"What else have you observed?"

Chloe seemed distracted for a moment. She was looking deep into the woods. They were in that area where she'd claimed to have seen the gray horse.

But just when he thought he'd lost her, she turned back to him and said, "About Alex? That he's not happy here."

He'd meant about himself—he wanted to know what Chloe thought about him—but her reference to Alex put him on edge. "My brother always thinks the grass is greener somewhere he's not."

"For him, maybe that's true."

"He can leave whenever he wants. I'm not tying him to the farm."

"There must be some reason he's staying."

"Money, pure and simple. When they retired and moved to North Carolina, our parents put the estate in a trust, with me as the head of the business for as long as I wanted to run it. Neither one of us can sell our share unless we both agree."

Thank God they had. If not, Damian feared he would have been looking for a job long ago instead of simply worrying about the possibility of having to do so.

"Alex seems to be pretty smart. I'm sure he's well educated, and he's certainly charming. He could get a job elsewhere."

"Yeah, he'd make a great car salesman," Damian said with a chuckle.

Chloe didn't laugh with him. Her forehead was pulled and she was biting the edge of her lower lip, as if she were trying to figure out something important.

Finally she said, "Maybe he doesn't want to leave so much as have more of a say in the business."

"We each serve our own functions."

"That might not be enough for Alex. Maybe he doesn't really want to leave you and Nissa, but maybe he needs to explore a new tunnel that he's not supposed to enter."

"Hah!"

Damian scoffed, but in his gut he knew Chloe could be right. Alex had always hated feeling like he had boundaries, and Damian couldn't get past putting up roadblocks. They might have matured, but their relationship hadn't really changed since they were kids.

"So where are these myriad entrances to the secret passageways?" Chloe asked.

Was she trying to keep him from asking her to analyze him? No longer certain he wanted her to do so, Damian went along with the distraction.

"There used to be a couple on each floor, but like I said, they're sealed off."

"The attic, too?"

"All of them are—"

"Hey, Dad! Chloe!" Nissa suddenly yelled. "Stop being so poky!"

Realizing how far ahead the girl had ridden, Damian urged Sarge into a lope, and Chloe did the same with her mount.

Having only been part of the household for a few days, Chloe certainly knew a lot about the place and people. Either she'd taken a lot of psychology courses and couldn't help analyzing everyone she met, or she had good reason to dig into their psyches.

Maybe both.

Digging too deep wouldn't be smart on her part. He couldn't have that. As much as he was attracted to her and liked her, if she learned too much about how he'd handled his business, he would simply be forced to get rid of her.

SO THE HOUSE HAD secret passageways, staircases and a tunnel, I mused. No wonder I'd been bothered by noises overhead at night. Someone had found his or her way inside and was stealing into the upper reaches of the house, rummaging around, searching for something.

The Equine Diamonds?

A logical explanation, I thought.

If so, the mystery person hadn't been Damian. He had free rein over his own home. Could Alex be searching under Damian's radar? I didn't think so. That would be contrary to how he operated.

As I thought about the potential suspects, I stood at the kitchen counter and scarfed down some leftovers for dinner. I was used to eating alone, so this wasn't unusual for me. When I'd rummaged through the refrigerator as Damian said I could, I'd looked over my shoulder expecting Mrs. Avery to show up, her expression disapproving as usual. No Mrs. Avery. Or anyone else for that matter.

Nissa had said the housekeeper was going to visit her nephew and the cook was simply going home. If only Merle had stuck around, just until Mrs. Avery was gone. I'd never yet found the opportunity to talk to her alone without interference. It had taken the housekeeper long enough to leave—more than an hour—but now I was truly alone and meant to make the most of my time in the empty house.

The lure of exploring secret passageways and a tunnel was great, but Damian had avoided telling me how many there were or where I might find them. Probably most of them were still sealed.

But *someone* had found a way in....

I had other things I wanted to investigate, so after taking my last bite of food and setting the dishes in the sink, I headed for the library.

It wasn't the computer that interested me this time. Not knowing what I was looking for, I started with the desk, which seemed to be the most logical place to find information. Nothing revealing in the top drawer or the ones on the right. But the big one on the left was in reality a file drawer. A look at the labels revealed my name.

I pulled the file and scanned the contents—basically my résumé and a letter that had been faxed from the agency. I found Dawn's, as well. The same. No home addresses—the agency was very careful to protect its employees' privacy—so there was no connection between me and Dawn here.

Every employee had a file, so I took them out, one at a time, and scanned the contents—mostly job applications and résumés. A few letters of recommendation and copies of letters written for various employees.

Remembering Alex's comment about Mrs. Avery being Priscilla's creature, I took special interest in the housekeeper's folder. No résumé. No application. Just a sheet with emergency information and a name that jumped out at me. Mrs. Avery's emergency contact was her nephew...*one Jack Larson!*

My mind raced. Jack wanted to get his hands on this

farm, and his aunt was working here. His very own spy? Definitely possible, and a reason for Mrs. Avery to continue to work for Damian even though Priscilla was gone. Speculating further, I wondered if it could be Jack ransacking the attic for those diamonds—the reason Mrs. Avery didn't want me going up there! She'd even been standing guard that first night.

Squirrels in the attic, indeed!

My hands shook with excitement as I replaced the file and scanned the remaining contents of the drawer.

One thick folder caught my interest. I pulled it out and realized I'd stumbled into Damian's private life. I almost returned it until I saw the folder had to do with his split from Priscilla....

Including divorce papers.

Glancing at the signatures—both parties had signed the document—I felt the weight on my shoulders lift slightly. I'd been half convinced that Priscilla was dead. But Damian had been telling the truth about the divorce. I'd let rumor and a child's fantasy get to me, and this legal document proved me wrong.

Replacing the folder, I felt almost giddy when I heard something scrape against floorboards high overhead.

Attic high.

Was someone up there now? Jack Larson?

I took a deep breath, determined to find out.

What if the person was dangerous, though? What if it was Jack and he'd been the one who'd tried to run me over the night before?

Dawn and I had taken an eight-week class in self-defense for women, but I wasn't comfortable with facing a potential enemy empty-handed. If Damian owned a gun, it wasn't in his desk. I looked around the room, my gaze stopping when it reached the fireplace. Quickly I crossed to it and lifted the iron poker from its hanger.

Armed, my pulse rushing through me faster than I could walk, I made my way out of the room and tiptoed up the stairs in the near dark. The sun had set, and without any more than night-lights, the rooms and hall and stairs were cast into deep shadows. As I reached the second floor, the sounds grew fainter as I drew nearer and then stopped. I didn't know whether or not to be disappointed that I'd missed the opportunity to find out who was frequenting the attic. Then again, just because I didn't hear anything didn't mean no one was there.

I crossed to the back of the house and crept up the attic stairs as silently as I could while focusing on any sound.

Nothing…

By the time I got to the top of the stairs, my heart steadied. I pressed my ear to the attic door and strained and strained to hear the slightest noise.

Nothing…

I took a breath, its deepness hindered a bit by my tension. And then I turned the knob.

Again, nothing!

The dratted door was locked!

Adrenaline pumped through me. One minute I was high, the next I felt ready to be scraped off the stairs. I reminded myself of what I'd found in the desk in the library. My evening hadn't gone to waste.

I knew Mrs. Avery was related to the man who

wanted to take over the farm. The same man who—according to Nissa—had been courting Dawn. The same man who'd denied being more than barely acquainted with Dawn and who had made overtures to me.

And along with that reasoning was knowing Damian had told me the truth about his divorce.

Still, fighting disappointment, I turned away from the attic door only to run straight into a very solid, very human, very masculine body.

Chapter Eleven

"What are you doing here?" I choked out as Damian's arms wound around my back and steadied me.

"I live here, remember?"

"You weren't supposed to be home tonight!"

"Is that why you're up here, sneaking around, carrying a poker?"

"I wasn't sneaking. I heard someone in the attic—and not for the first time, let me tell you—but the door is locked."

"Locked? The door is never locked."

"Well, it is now. And I brought the poker to protect myself."

But how could I protect myself from the master of the house? I wondered as his arms tightened around me and his expression intensified.

I wanted to protest…to tell him to let me go…

…to tell him not to…

I had trouble breathing and I wondered if he could tell. His eyelids lowered to half-mast and his expression held a hunger that thrilled me to my toes. A hunger that I recognized myself and turned my knees to mush.

"Ah, Chloe…"

Damian sounded as breathless as I, and when his head dipped so that his lips met mine, I dropped the poker and lifted my arms to twine around his neck. My mouth opened and he wasted no time before exploring every crevice. I kissed him back with everything I had.

Unable to deny myself any longer, I gave into the attraction that had been growing since I'd arrived. I let myself float on a cloud of growing desire. When his hands moved up my spine and around my sides to the fullness of my breasts, I welcomed the sensation that heated me through to my core.

Knowing that he'd told me the truth about Priscilla freed me of suspicion. Damian was exactly what he seemed to be—the kind of man I needed in my life.

When his thumbs caught my nipples through the thin material of my blouse, I moaned and moved closer so that my body fit tight against his. I felt his legs shift slightly…his erection now snugged into me.

For one sweet moment I imagined what it would be like to feel that hard length inside me…

Then laughter drifted up the stairs.

The realization that Nissa and Alex were below hit me like a bucket of cold water. I tore my mouth from Damian's and twisted free of his body. My breath was shaky, as was his, but I could see the effort he made to get control of himself. Before my eyes he withdrew into the aloof Damian I'd first met.

"I need to see to Nissa. Her stomach was bothering her. That's why we came home early."

Instantly concerned, I said, "I'll make some tea—that should help."

"I can take care of my daughter."

Shocked by the dismissal, I stood there on the attic landing staring after him as he made a quick exit without so much as a kind word for me. I took deep breaths until I was as calm as he seemed to be. Then I picked up the poker and descended to my bedroom. I would leave the makeshift weapon there until later so I wouldn't have to explain why I was returning it to the library to Alex or Nissa.

What in the world had just happened? One minute Damian was kissing me, the next he was giving me the cold shoulder.

I glanced at myself in the mirror. My skin was flushed—not merely my face, but my neck and the swell of my breasts, as well. My hair was mussed and my blouse seemed disheveled. I spent a few minutes getting myself together, but even when the sexual flush faded altogether, I had no desire to go downstairs to face Damian.

What was I going to do about him?

I pondered the question as I stared out the window into the twilight.

Damian was my employer, and I was here under false pretenses. Even if he wasn't regretting kissing me now—which, indeed, I thought he was—even if he wanted something more between us, was it really possible? If he knew the real reason I was here, that Dawn was my foster sister and best friend, and that I had arrived thinking he might have had something to do with her disappearance, how would he react? No doubt he would become cold and distant. And no doubt he would fire me.

Not that I believed Damian had harmed Dawn.

Troubled, I focused on the grounds and copse of trees leading to the palisades and wished for an answer.

As if my thoughts had reached out to the beyond, a pale shape separated from the trees and stood in the open, graceful neck lifting toward my window. The gray horse snorted and bobbed his head, then danced around for a moment as if it were waiting for me….

I couldn't resist. I raced down the servants' stairs into the kitchen.

Part of me wanted to call Damian and tell him to see the gray for himself. But the other part—the part he'd wounded by cutting me off—didn't want another encounter until I'd had time to put what had happened into perspective.

I made a quiet escape out the back door.

The horse was waiting impatiently, snorting and pawing the ground. I approached slowly, my eyes devouring the pale shadow against the gloom of twilight.

Was this horse real?

My imagination?

Or was it truly a ghost horse?

"Hey, boy, what's up?" I called softly as I glided toward him in my most nonaggressive manner.

He whickered and snorted and danced himself right into the woods.

"No, wait!"

Though I ran, I couldn't keep up with him. Determined not to lose him, I did my best, pushed myself to go faster. But fate wasn't with me. Dodging trees, my ghost horse kept gaining ground until all I could see of him was a shimmer in the dark woods.

Winded, I tottered to a stop and sucked in big gulps of damp night air. I never took my eyes from the path, but soon I could make out nothing but mist rising from the ground. Keeping my focus on the spot where I'd lost him, I moved ahead, anyway, hoping against hope that I would see him again.

Obviously, he wanted me to.

Why? That was the question.

He appeared to me and no other. Nissa had spied him from her bedroom window, but she'd never gotten close to him. The last time I'd seen him, he'd led me to the exact spot where Dawn had lost her hair clip. This time he'd waited for me to come from my bedroom. So why had he disappeared so suddenly? Where had he meant to lead me today?

As a matter of fact...*where was I?*

I stopped short and looked around. I'd never come so deep into these woods. The other times I'd cut through them simply to get to the palisades. I didn't recognize anything. I wasn't even sure how to retrace my steps in the quickly falling darkness.

I was lost.

And without a flashlight.

No sooner had that occurred to me than I heard the crunch of twigs. This was no horse coming toward me, I thought, backing up the way I had come. These were human footfalls.

My back rammed into something hard. Gasping, I

whipped around to glare at a tree in my path. Quickly I skirted it and flew back the way I had come—or so I hoped.

The crunch of footsteps followed.

Is that why the horse had disappeared? Because someone else was here?

Fanciful imaginings, but what part of this woman-horse relationship seemed real?

I forced myself to move faster. Trees loomed massive all around me. I got through them somehow—like a bat relying on its radar—and eventually the whickering of happily pastured horses secured my direction.

By the time I fell out of the copse of trees into the open near the house, my heart was thundering and I felt faint with relief. I made for the back door and only when I got there did I glance back and try to pierce the darkness.

I could swear I saw movement at the edge of the woods, but if someone was there—if, indeed, I had been followed—the person didn't follow me out into the open.

Trembling now, I took refuge in the house.

Voices carried from the parlor or library—which, I couldn't be certain. But both were male, so I assumed Damian and Alex were arguing about something again. Still wanting to avoid Damian, I kept to the back stairs and sought refuge in my bedroom.

Immediately the room's unusual warmth soothed the damp chill from me, and I realized someone had lit the logs in the fireplace. Who? I wondered, as flames danced shadows across the walls.

Damian? Perhaps he'd come to see me and, not finding me in my room, had lit the fire as a peace offering?

A different kind of warmth spread through me at the thought. I wanted to believe in his kindness. I wanted to believe in the passionate man who'd kissed me weak-kneed. I didn't like the other Damian, the one who could be cold and rude, the one who reminded me of my father when I'd displeased him. The father who'd so easily abandoned me.

I stood at the closed windows for a moment and looked out, but there was no movement below. No horse. No man. Maybe I'd imagined being followed, I thought, suddenly feeling exhausted. And why wouldn't I, with stress being my constant companion? Surely my escalating stress was the reason for the tightness across my forehead. I rubbed at my temples for a moment, then changed out of my clothes and into my nightgown. A shower would have to wait until morning. I was simply too exhausted to do anything but crawl into bed.

My head whirled as I scooted under the covers and let myself drift to another place....

A shimmer through the dark catches my gaze, and I think the ghost horse returns. But when the shimmer draws closer, it takes the form of a woman.

"Dawn, I've found you!"

She smiles sadly at me and reaches out, but no matter how far I run, I get no closer.

I hear a whicker, and her sad smile melts into despair. She blinks and a single tear rolls down each cheek.

"Why are you crying?" I ask.

She looks behind her as another shimmer of light takes form. The ghost horse. He jumps as if frightened, then reaches upward with thrashing front legs.

Dawn turns back to me, her face now wet with tears, her expression pleading...begging me to understand....

I awoke in a sweat, my head throbbing as I tossed and turned and tried to find a position that would make me feel better. The headache was bad enough, but now my stomach felt unsettled. I remembered that Damian had said Nissa's stomach was upset. Something we both ate? Maybe she'd snacked from the refrigerator before going out. Nausea forced me from the warm bed. Thinking I would go downstairs to find some peppermint tea, I headed for the door.

But with the first few steps, my head went light and I faltered.

The door suddenly seemed to be a long, long way to go. I forced one foot forward and then the other, concentrating all the while on the doorknob, which went in and out of focus.

I reached for it...connected...turned...

And then just as the door opened, my world whirled around me and I felt myself falling....

"IT WOULDN'T HURT to sell off the old Bosch Barns acreage," Alex said. "That wasn't originally part of the farm and we don't need the extra land."

Damian sipped at a brandy and stared into the fire as if it held answers for him. "Jack Larson doesn't want the land for himself. He wants to make money off it by reselling it to developers."

"Then cut out the middle man. I'll find developers who would pay top price."

"The idea is to keep the developers out!"

Damian couldn't believe he was having this conversation with his brother. He needed to be alone, needed time to think about what had happened between him and Chloe. About what he was going to do about it. About her.

"You can't freeze Graylord Pastures in a time warp, Damian. It's the twenty-first century."

"I like things the way they are. I won't sell off the farm a piece at a time until there isn't anything left."

"No, you'll chance losing everything at once instead. Half of the estate is mine, Damian. Father left it in trust to you, because he thought you were the one with all the sense. You were the one who would keep it in the black. What a joke!"

"We've had some bad luck," Damian admitted. "But we've made it through bad luck before."

"Not enough to require a second mortgage."

"You know why I had to take it," Damian said, silently cursing Priscilla.

"You didn't *have* to."

Damian faced his brother and asked, "What would be *your* alternative?"

"What does it matter? You never consider my ideas, anyway. There's no talking to you! There never was!"

Alex turned on his heel and strode out of the library, leaving Damian to his dark thoughts. He would curse the day he met Priscilla...but if he hadn't met her, he wouldn't have Nissa.

His daughter had said she'd felt better before going off to her room, but Damian thought perhaps he ought to check on her and then retire for the evening himself.

He was leaving the library when he heard a soft thump overhead.

What the hell was that?

As he neared the stairs, he realized the lights were still on in the kitchen. He detoured to turn them off, then took the back stairs up to the second floor.

He had to pass Chloe's room on the way to his daughter's. He steeled himself to walk by without hesitating. Only by chance did he realize Chloe's door was cracked open and that something white was fluttering out into the hall—a ribbon.

He stopped and touched the door. "Chloe."

Then he saw her sprawled out on the floor and rushed inside. Her falling was the thump he'd heard a few minutes ago, the ribbon one streaming from her nightgown. Kneeling next to her, he put fingers to the artery in her neck. Her pulse was thready.

"Chloe, can you hear me?" Gently he shook her shoulder. "Chloe, wake up."

She moaned. Her head moved and her lashes fluttered open. Her eyes were pale gray pools of confusion.

"Damian?" she whispered.

"Do you think anything might be broken?" When she moved her limbs and shook her head, he said, "Then, let me help you up."

He scooped an arm behind her. She tried to get to her feet, but she was weak and woozy, so in the end he simply lifted her into his arms. A wave of protectiveness washed over him, and reluctantly he placed her in the bed and let go of her.

"What happened?"

"Exhausted…slept for a while…then woke with a headache." She put a hand to her stomach. "I wanted tea…dizzy…"

Damian glanced at the fireplace. He didn't like the color of the flames. Too yellow. Quickly, he opened the windows to let in fresh air. "So you passed out before you got out the door?"

Chloe merely moaned again.

"I'm getting you to an emergency room."

Ignoring her protests, he picked her up again, grabbed the coverlet, then rushed her down the stairs and out to the car.

By the time he got her in the passenger seat, she was protesting. "Damian, I'm feeling better already."

"That's because you're getting fresh air." He wrapped the coverlet around her and closed her door. Once in the driver's seat, he said, "If I'm right, you're going to need oxygen."

"Oxygen?" she echoed. "Why?"

"I think you got some carbon monoxide poisoning. You shouldn't have started that fire. The chimney must be blocked."

"I didn't…I thought *you* did."

"I didn't, either."

Then who the hell had? he wondered as he sped north toward Galena. Alex hadn't gone upstairs. Besides, he would have known to check the flue. It wasn't likely that Nissa had gotten out of bed and started a fire for Chloe, either. And no one else was home.

Then he remembered what Chloe had said about her

being on the attic stairs—that she'd heard someone in the attic and it hadn't been the first time.

Damian called Alex on his cell phone, told him where they were headed and asked him to put out the fire and check the chimney. When he got home, he would check out the attic himself for signs of some mysterious intruder.

Chloe was too quiet. Because she was that ill or because her mind was on the same track as his?

"How are you doing?"

"Better," she said to his relief.

But when they got to the emergency room, the doctor who checked Chloe concurred with Damian's thoughts about the oxygen therapy. Damian intended to wait right by Chloe's side, but the doctor insisted she be checked in overnight for observation. He told Damian to go home, get some sleep and come back for Chloe at noon the next day.

Wanting to check things out at the house for himself, Damian didn't argue. He hated leaving Chloe there by herself and told her so.

"Nice to know you care."

Her words were soft yet laced with something else that touched him, made him remember how he'd left her on the stairs after kissing her, after touching her….

"I do care, Chloe."

He did. He hadn't known how much until he'd found her passed out on the floor. Until then, he'd merely thought she was good for Nissa and had put his attraction to her as not having had a woman in his life since Priscilla. But when he'd seen her so vulnerable…

"I'd better get going now."

She nodded and softly said, "Thank you for saving my life."

Her life…

She could have died. Carbon monoxide poisoning was nothing to mess with. Luckily she'd gotten the door open at least a crack. Luckily he'd found her only a short time after she'd passed out. But who had built the fire, and why, were still question marks in his mind.

Driving home, he wondered if one person could really be so unlucky. Falling and hitting her head. Nearly being run over by a car. Breathing poison into her system.

Something told him more than bad luck was at work.

Something told him that someone wanted Chloe gone…one way or the other.

Chapter Twelve

I had a lot of time to think in that hospital bed. I slept some, thought more. Hard not to do when nurses or technicians kept waking me up, supposedly to take vitals—no doubt to make sure I was still alive.

I could have died if Damian hadn't found me…that was very clear to me.

Why was not.

Who wanted me gone so desperately that they were ready to harm me if I wouldn't leave Graylord Pastures?

They'd just removed the oxygen and I was breathing fine on my own, when I saw a bouquet of flowers enter the hospital room followed by a visitor. For a moment I stopped breathing altogether.

"I thought you could use some company and an apology," Jack Larson said.

Shocked by his unexpected appearance, I didn't know what to say to him in return, so I merely blinked and forced my lungs to work again.

"I'll just put these over here," he said, setting the flowers on the windowsill. Then he moved closer to my bed—too close for my comfort.

My mind racing, I asked, "How did you know I was hospitalized?"

"News gets around fast in this part of the state."

No doubt his aunt had told him. I wondered what other information Mrs. Avery shared with her nephew about the goings-on at Graylord Pastures.

"I'm fine now. As a matter of fact I'll be going home in a little while."

He looked at me pointedly. "Home? Or back to Graylord Pastures?"

There it was—his reason for coming to see me. "Damian will be here to pick me up soon." Though I tried to keep hostility out of my tone, I wasn't sure I succeeded.

"Is that an invitation for me to leave?"

Not that he moved an inch closer to the door.

"I need to get dressed," I told him civilly.

"So, an apology is no good from me?"

"For what exactly are you apologizing?"

"I'm not really sure. For whatever put you off the other night."

We were at an impasse. I wasn't going to share my suspicions. Apparently, he wasn't going to go into his true intentions.

"Perhaps this isn't the best time, after what you've been through and all," he finally said.

"No, it isn't."

"Another time, then. *If* you're still working for Graylord, that is."

He left, leaving me wondering if that was some kind of veiled threat.

I got out of the hospital bed and went to the door,

wanting to make certain Jack had actually left. I didn't see him in the busy hallway, so I relaxed a little. Unfortunately, I couldn't get dressed until Damian arrived with a change of clothing. I didn't relish the idea of leaving the hospital in a nightgown and blanket.

I sat on the edge of the bed and waited. More time to think. I've never been a coward, but for a moment I wondered if I shouldn't pack my bags and go back to Chicago.

That would mean abandoning Dawn—and Nissa. I just couldn't.

Bizarrely enough, I didn't know which was more frightening—the physical danger I found myself in…or the emotional. My growing feelings for Damian were pretty potent.

When he arrived at the hospital a short while later, my emotions were mixed. I was glad to see him, thankful that he'd saved my life, dreading his learning my true purpose here, and confused about his feelings for me.

Damian had said he "cared." Not very specific.

And he didn't repeat the sentiment when he gave me my clothing—a calf-length flowered skirt and short-sleeved pink blouse—or a while later when he took me out to the car and started for home. He didn't notice the flowers on the windowsill and I didn't say anything. I left them there, thinking the nurses could do whatever they wanted with the bouquet.

Damian simply talked about my taking it easy for the day and warned me to tell him if I was feeling off or having any unexpected side effects. Nothing personal.

We were well on our way to Graylord Pastures before he brought up the actual incident.

"Alex checked the chimney last night to find out why your room was filled with carbon monoxide. He found the flue was blocked."

"How?"

"The fireplace was in use all last winter, so the blockage could be natural. It wouldn't normally be used again till fall when it would be checked out first."

It was "in use." Not "Dawn had used it." He was still avoiding talking about her, too.

As to whether this incident had really been an accident was open to question in my mind. "So did you find out who started the fire?"

He shook his head. "No one was home but family. Mrs. Avery didn't get back until after I returned from the hospital, and Merle spent the night at her sister's."

"What about one of the barn workers?"

"They don't have keys to the house."

"But someone got into the attic without anyone knowing." *Anyone but me.*

"Last night I went up and looked around the attic for myself. Not that there was anything to see. Not specifically, that is."

"What does that mean?"

"Someone had been going through things—old furniture, trunks. That was obvious because the dust was disturbed. But for years Nissa has gone up there to amuse herself. She likes to rummage through the family history."

"Has she been up there lately?"

"She says not."

"Well, someone has."

"Who, then?"

How much could I say without revealing all I'd figured out in the last few days?

"How about...someone interested in finding the Equine Diamonds?"

Damian's visage darkened. "Alex talks too much. That's nothing but an old tale, as far as I'm concerned. We don't know the diamonds even exist anymore." His irritation came through loud and clear.

"Whether they do or not, someone could be searching for them...someone desperate to score big."

"You wouldn't have a theory about who that might be?" he asked.

"What about Jack Larson?"

Damian chanced a quick glance away from the road to me. "What about him?" he asked, scowling.

"I know he'd like what you have. I heard him ask about buying one of your stallions. And then in Galena, he just happened to run into me, and—"

"What! Why didn't you tell me this before?"

I ignored the heated question and told him, "Jack came to see me in the hospital this morning, too. He wanted to know if I was staying on. The other night he was feeling me out about what was going on here—whether or not there were any more disasters. Though, now that I think about it, I don't know why he needed to come on to me when all he had to do was ask his aunt. No doubt she told him where to find me."

TMI...too much information. My stomach lurched as I expected Damian to ask me how I knew Mrs. Avery was Jack Larson's aunt. Lucky for me he didn't seem to digest that I had not-so-common knowledge about one of his employees.

"You think Larson is really after the diamonds?" he asked. "And that Mrs. Avery is helping him?"

"You don't think it's possible?"

"I think you've been doing a lot of imagining about the situation, considering you've only been here for less than a week."

"A lot has happened in a few days." I'd had enough excitement for a lifetime. "So, if you don't think Jack Larson is rummaging around in the attic, then who?"

Damian's jaw tightened, but he didn't answer. I could swear he'd thought of someone else, hence the descent into silence. He was pushing me away again, just as he'd done the evening before. I felt closed off, suddenly alone. Graylord Pastures was a welcome sight.

As was Nissa when she came running out of the house to the car. The moment I alighted, she threw her arms around me.

"I thought you weren't ever coming back."

I hugged her, saying, "I'm okay, and nothing could keep me from coming back."

Hollow words. Someone was trying to keep me from Nissa. They just hadn't succeeded.

Yet…

Even once inside the house, Nissa clung to me. Alex volunteered to get me anything I needed, and Merle told me she would cook whatever caught my fancy. Everyone in the household fussed over me, other than Mrs. Avery. Big surprise. And Damian. He was exceptionally quiet, as if his mind were elsewhere.

Dwelling on Jack Larson or someone else who could be after the Equine Diamonds?

Since he wouldn't tell me who he suspected, I guessed it would have to be someone close to him… like his brother. But Alex had been gone with Damian and Nissa the evening before. Or had he? He'd taken his own car. Maybe he'd been the first to return and had gotten himself into the attic without my knowing. Perhaps the secret passageways weren't still sealed, after all.

I rested, as instructed, and accepted all the attention for a couple of hours, after which I grew bored and restless. I had to get out of the house where I could think.

"I'm going for a walk," I announced, getting up off the couch, where I'd been paging through a horse magazine.

Nissa popped up off the floor, where she'd been keeping me company. "I'll go with you."

"Alone." I smoothed back the wild red hair from her cheek. "I'll be fine, I promise. I just want to walk over to the pastures and watch the horses for a while. I need fresh air." Before she could volunteer again, I added, "And a little solitude."

Nissa didn't appear happy, but neither did she object.

Even though the walk was short, it did me good to stretch my legs. And it did my soul good to watch the horses in the pasture—a mare with her foal and a juvenile that appeared to be hers, as well, if the similar markings were any indication.

Clifford was just turning out another couple of mares, both of whom looked to be pregnant. When he saw me, he came over to where I stood.

"Heard you had a scare last night."

"A big one," I said.

"Mr. Damian have an explanation for what happened to you?"

"I'm afraid not."

His narrow face pulled into a scowl and he looked down his hawkish nose at me. "You're lucky he didn't send you packing."

"I'm not the one who did anything wrong."

"You saying someone did?"

Not wanting to go there, I looked over the groom's shoulder and changed the subject. "Such beautiful horses. And I love riding out here."

"You're not bad for a city woman, neither," Clifford admitted. "Probably as good as the last one."

"You mean Dawn?"

"Yup. She would've ridden every horse in the place if Mr. Damian would've let her."

Now why hadn't I thought to ask the groom about her before? "It makes sense that he's particular who rides which horses. I mean, they are very valuable animals," I said, wondering what I could learn from him.

Clifford nodded. "Only him and Mr. Alex ride the stallions. Well, that he knows of. One night when I worked late, I caught Miss Dawn riding one of 'em out in the far pasture. Bareback, too."

"A stallion?" My pulse fluttered, and I tried to keep my voice casual when I asked, "Which one?"

"Oh, he's not here now. Got himself killed, poor Centaur did."

"Dawn rode Centaur?"

"You heard of him, huh? Yeah, just that once. Well, that's all she admitted to. But I seen her quite a few times making over that fella, bringing him apples and carrots. She was in love with that gray, and I swear he must've loved her, too. He weren't no easy ride, but you'd a thought he was if you'd seen *her* on his back. Gentle as a lamb he was. Never seen nothing like it. Like they had some kinda otherworldly connection."

My chest squeezed tight, and my blood rushed through my veins double-time.

Dawn and Centaur…both dead and still connected? Is that why I saw them both in my dreams?

It couldn't be…or maybe it could.

MY WHOLE DAY was off-kilter. After my walk I felt exhausted, so I made myself comfortable on the parlor sofa, thinking I would rest until dinner. I could hardly keep my eyes open. I didn't fight it. I let myself drift off.

When I awoke, it was hours later. The parlor was dark but for a table light set on low. And someone had covered me with an afghan.

Damian?

Was he capable of such a small but comforting gesture?

Realizing I'd slept right through dinner, I wandered into the kitchen in search of leftovers.

Merle turned from where she was cleaning a counter. "Ah, there you are, miss. I fixed a plate for you."

"Bless your heart, Merle. Suddenly I'm ravenous."

"Good," she said, pulling a plate out of the refrigerator and setting it in the microwave. "It didn't get a chance to get cold, so it'll only take a minute. Set yourself down." She indicated a stool at a raised counter.

"You don't have to wait on me."

"Sit."

I sat and she poured me a tall glass of iced tea, and I realized I finally had that opportunity to talk to her alone—the first time since arriving at the farm. For once, Mrs. Avery was nowhere around.

"Thanks." Hoping the housekeeper could stay away just for ten minutes, I said, "Merle, what did you think of my predecessor?"

"Miss Dawn? A very dramatic young woman, but good-hearted. And good for Miss Nissa."

"Do you think what they said about her is true? I mean about her eloping?"

The microwave dinged. Merle shrugged and went for the plate of food. "She was always talking about men liking her, and she talked a good game, but I never got the idea that she was seriously attached to any *one* man."

I wanted to ask about Jack Larson, but I thought that might be pushing it a bit. Merle undoubtedly had certain loyalties to the housekeeper.

"Mmm, smells delicious," I murmured as the cook set down a plate of chicken and dumplings and sweet potatoes. "What about the night she, um…left." I'd almost said *disappeared.* "Was she nervous? Happy?"

Merle gave me a curious expression. "Just her usual self. Why are you so interested?"

"Just curious. I was down by the barns earlier. Clifford said Dawn used to come down there, too. He said she had a real connection with some of the horses."

Merle nodded. "When she left the house that last night, it was to go down to the barns. She did that most evenings. Took some carrots or apples with her for some of the horses. I thought it was a bit late that night, but she said she couldn't sleep."

I'd started eating while she was talking, but my attention didn't waver. "How late?"

"Well after ten. I always stay late before my days off to prepare meals that can just be thrown in the oven or reheated when I'm gone. I was taking an extra day, so there was extra cooking to do. I was just finishing up and getting ready to leave when she came downstairs."

"This is delicious," I said, swallowing a piece of dumpling. I washed it down with some iced tea. "So you were gone when all the excitement happened."

Merle suddenly grew tight-lipped. A little thrill shot through me at her reaction.

"What is it?" I asked, fork poised over the food.

"Just thinking about that poor horse. I know Miss Dawn was extra fond of him."

"Centaur? What about him?"

"The accident was such a tragedy and all. It had to be an accident."

It sounded like Merle was trying to convince herself of the fact. "I…I don't understand."

"When I came back from my days off, they were both gone."

My chest suddenly squeezed tight and I could hardly get the next words out. "When exactly did Centaur die?"

"The same night Miss Dawn left."

It hit me then like a full-force gale. Dawn had gone

out to see the horses…Centaur, no doubt…a sudden storm came up and the stallion got out of the pasture and died…and by the next morning, Dawn was gone.

There had to be a connection!

A chill spread through me.

Had Dawn ridden the horse that night? Had she been responsible for his getting loose? Is that why Merle had been so reluctant to say anything—because she'd put it together, too? I'd found the hair clip at the palisades. Had Dawn gone after the stallion to try to take him back only to see him rush over the bluff to his death?

If so, Dawn would never forgive herself. I knew her well enough to understand that if, indeed, she'd been even remotely responsible for the stallion's death she would never be able to face the Graylords again.

Was that it, then?

The real reason Dawn had made up an elopement and left without saying goodbye to anyone?

The real reason she hadn't contacted me since?

Because she'd feared being held responsible for a tragedy she hadn't meant to instigate?

I understood all but her not contacting me to let me know what had happened. To let me know that she was all right. Dawn should have known that *I* wouldn't judge her. That I would have backed her up and done whatever I could to get her out of this mess.

I couldn't help but be relieved that my foster sister and best friend might still be alive and unharmed and in hiding…and couldn't help wondering if once again I'd been abandoned by someone I loved.

I realized Merle was staring at me—because I wasn't eating or because she'd been waiting for a response to what she'd told me? I pulled myself together, picked up my fork and took a small bite of chicken.

"Nissa really misses Dawn," I said.

"But now she has you."

Merle seemed relieved, no doubt because I didn't press her further. I doubted that she'd told Damian as much as she'd just told me.

The more I thought about it, though, the less sure I was of how the Centaur-Dawn scenario had played out that night. Definitely, there had to be a connection. But if Dawn had arranged her disappearing act and if no one else was involved, then why was someone trying to drive *me* away from the place? And how did someone searching the attic fit in with the rest?

"Well, I'm done here," Merle said, "as soon as I wash your plate and glass."

"No, go. I'll do it."

"All right, then. I'm off the next couple of days. You won't go leaving without telling anyone, will you?"

Nearly choking on my mouthful of food, I somehow got it down. "I'm not planning on leaving anytime soon."

"Good girl." Merle patted my shoulder as she walked by me to the back door.

Left to myself, I made quick work of the food and cleaned up as I'd promised, then wondered what I was going to do with myself now that I was rested and fueled. I needed a distraction until I could look at what Merle had told me in the cold light of morning. I could read if I had a book that interested me. Surely something on the library shelves would do.

Was Damian holed up in the library? I wondered. My pulse was doing a dance at the thought of running into him. Which would he be tonight—the Damian who heated my blood with passion or the one who left me chilled and uncertain?

Before I could make myself move in that direction, I heard a shriek that came from outside the house. I rushed to the back door and flung it open. The night was clear and the moon cast a blue glow over the earth.

"Wa-a-ait!" echoed through the night at me.

My gaze snapped to a nearby copse of trees, where a bobbing light preceded a slender figure.

"Nissa!" I called out.

What in the world was she doing outside running into the woods? Without thinking, I set out after her.

"Nissa!" I called again, "Stop right there!" but either the girl didn't hear or was ignoring me.

Thankfully my legs were longer than hers, I was well rested and seemed to have no ill aftereffects from the carbon monoxide. The distance between us quickly narrowed. The beam from her flashlight bobbed, and I swore it picked up something moving ahead of her. Something or someone.

I had just about caught up to her when Nissa stumbled and shrieked. The flashlight flew from her hand, hitting the ground at the same time she did.

I was on her in seconds.

"Are you all right?" I gasped, realizing I was out of breath.

Nissa was already flying to her feet. I caught her arm and she struggled with me.

"Let me go. I have to go!"

I didn't loosen my grip. "Go where?"

"After her!"

"You can't run into the woods at night!"

"I saw her!" Nissa shrieked, striking me, elbow to head, in her struggle to free herself.

"Ahh!" I fell back and would have fallen if not for the tree that caught me. For a moment I was seeing stars that weren't in the sky.

"Chloe! I'm sorry! I didn't mean to hurt you. I didn't!" A frantic Nissa was trying to grab on to me.

"I…I'll be all right. Give me a minute."

"She'll get away." Nissa sobbed and stared into the dark.

I put my arms around her. "Who will get away? Nissa, who were you following?"

"M-my mother's ghost."

Chapter Thirteen

"Let's get out of here." I hugged Nissa tight and let her sob against my chest for a moment. My throat tightened, and my eyes stung in empathy. How many times had I cried like this over the loss of my own mother? "We'll go back to the house and talk. Okay?"

She nodded and forced out a muffled "Okay."

Praying that Nissa wouldn't bolt on me, I let go of her and fetched the flashlight she'd dropped. Then I took her hand, laced my fingers through hers and started back for the house. Nissa came along without a struggle. She sniffled and wiped away her tears with her free hand. Several times on the way, she glanced behind her, as if hoping to spot the ghost.

When I got her into the house, I took her straight upstairs to her room. She was trembling, and I thought she could use a minute to pull herself together.

"Why don't you change for bed and then we'll talk." Thinking she'd want some privacy, I turned around and crossed the room. "I'll just go look at your fish."

Once again I was transfixed by the beauty of the tank with its pretty hidey-holes for the colorful fish, one of which amused me as it spewed sparkly gravel in every direction. Some of the bigger translucent chunks looked too big for the little fish to move. Which just proved that if you have enough determination, you can do anything.

I could hear Nissa moving around behind me, climbing into her pajamas. And sniffling.

Wanting to distract her a bit, I asked, "Did you put the fish tank together yourself?"

"Dad helped me with the stuff like the tank itself and the filters, but I picked out the fish and everything in it."

"Great job. It's beautiful."

"Thanks. You can turn around now."

Nissa looked so young and vulnerable sitting on the edge of her bed that I joined her and put an arm around her back. "Now…tell me what happened."

She took a deep breath and said, "I was down by the barns with Dad checking on one of the pregnant mares. She was okay, so he told me to come back here to get ready for bed. That's when I saw someone come around the other side of the house."

"Why did you think it was your mom's ghost?"

"I…I saw her. I used my flashlight, but she took off through the w-woods and I did, too. Then you came."

Nissa blinked and tears rolled down her cheeks again. I didn't know what to say, so I hugged her again. Sometimes that's all someone needed—another person to listen and a comforting pair of arms. How much of a look had Nissa gotten with the flashlight? The figure could have been anyone…possibly the person who'd been rifling through the attic.

"You believe me, don't you?" Nissa asked.

"I saw someone, too," I hedged.

"But you don't think it was Mom's ghost, do you?"

A week ago I would have said I didn't believe in ghosts, but circumstances had changed the way I thought.

"I don't know," I said honestly, though a flesh-and-blood person seemed far more likely than a spirit. "But I believe in *you,* Nissa."

The girl wrapped her arms around my waist and buried her head in the hollow at my shoulder. We stayed that way, neither of us saying anything, for a long while. My heart went out to Nissa, and I felt closer to her emotionally than I had to anyone in a long time.

Anyone since Dawn.

Eventually the excitement caught up to the girl, and I realized she was getting sleepy. I pulled the covers down and scooted her under them.

"Pleasant dreams," I murmured, turning out the bedside light.

Once out of her room, I went in search of Damian so that I could tell him what had happened. He'd told me he wanted to know about any incident that had to do with his daughter immediately, and I figured this qualified.

He wasn't in the house, so he must still have been at one of the barns. Flashlight in hand, I set out to find him, which proved to be an easy task. I simply followed the raised voices into the far barn. Damian sounded really angry, so I stopped just inside the door and stayed in the shadows to listen.

"I want to know whenever someone who doesn't belong steps foot on Graylord Pastures' land!"

"Now you want me playing security cop?" Theo answered, sounding equally angry.

"Unless you want to be personally responsible if more feed disappears. This latest theft is going to set us back thousands!"

I started at the realization that something else had gone wrong on the farm. Jack Larson had just been asking me if there had been any new crises. As if he had known…

"It's not my fault that you've made your own enemies," Theo grumbled.

"If I've done anything to make someone strike back, I don't know who, or what I did."

"What about Priscilla? You think what you did to her was fair?"

My pulse picked up at the mention of Damian's ex-wife.

"What are you saying, Theo? You think she's behind all the bad things that have been happening to us?"

When the barn manager said, "I'm just giving you an example of someone who would have reason to hate you!" I didn't get the feeling that he was too fond of Damian himself.

"My divorce might not have been amicable, but I can't see Priscilla trying to ruin me. Then how could she get more money out of me?"

"Think what you will," Theo said, sounding as though Damian was a fool. "Now, if you don't mind, I need to get out of here and get home."

Theo stalked through the barn, so preoccupied with his own thoughts that he didn't seem to notice me in the shadows.

Outside, he got into his truck and drove off.

Great. Now I had to give Damian more bad news. Part of me wanted to run the other way, but the other part figured he didn't need to be alone now, either.

I crossed through the barn, noticing most of the stalls were empty because the horses were pastured. Damian was spreading a blanket across a couple of bales of fresh hay in one of the empty stalls.

"Planning on sleeping here tonight?"

Damian started and whipped around so that his hostile gaze met mine. Then he took a deep breath and blinked the hostility away.

"Funny Valentine is overdue," he explained. "Gestation isn't precise—but usually no longer than a year. Valentine is past that by a week. I want to be here in case she needs me."

"Nissa said the mare was all right."

"She seems to be, but I'm being cautious, just in case."

"Wouldn't keeping an eye on her at night be Theo's job?"

"He and Alex and I take turns."

I hesitated only a second before saying, "I heard the argument, you know. I was back there." I indicated the entry to the barn. "So, there's been more bad luck?"

"Thousands of dollars of feed stolen. Someone backed a truck right up to the feed shed and took it."

"And no one heard the vehicle?"

"It must have happened when I was at the hospital with you. Alex was in the house dealing with the fireplace. Theo was back at his place for the night."

"I'm sorry."

"It's not your fault."

"What do the authorities say?"

"They haven't been out here yet. It's not a critical situation, so someone will be out in the morning. But truth be told, I doubt they'll get my feed back. Or even find the culprit. What are you doing out here, anyway? You should be resting. Not wandering around."

That he sounded like he cared warmed me through, made me even sadder that I had to give him more bad news.

"I'm fine, Damian. Rested. No ill effects. Like new. But something happened.... I had to talk to you."

He stepped closer and closed his hands around my upper arms. "What now? Did someone else try to hurt you?"

Heat spread from his palms through my blouse to my flesh, distracting me. He sounded so concerned. And his intense expression thrilled me. It made me think he did care...at least about my welfare.

I mentally shook myself. This was about his daughter, not about me.

"Nissa...she's all right. But she thought she saw Priscilla's ghost." I quickly told him about the race through the copse.

Damian cursed under his breath and let go of me. "I wish Nissa would get it out of her head that her mother's dead."

"She would if you'd let her *see* Priscilla. Nissa isn't the only one who thinks your ex-wife is dead. There are rumors that she just disappeared, that she met with foul play." I wasn't going to tell him that Theo had been one of the people to suggest as much. Considering the conclusions my talk with Merle had led me to, I said, "And more rumors about the real reason Dawn disappeared in the middle of the night."

The last was a bit of an embellishment, but I got what I was looking for.

Seeming truly puzzled, he said, "Dawn left a note, for God's sake!"

Which made me think that he really believed it. "A note that was written after she was gone."

"What are you talking about?"

"I was looking for anything Dawn might have left in the computer," I said, hoping he would think I meant the lesson plans. "And I found the note. I read it. The date on the file was wrong. Dawn's supposed goodbye was written the day after she disappeared."

I wished I could tell him everything. The whole truth. But I wasn't foolish enough to believe he would let my lies go. I would be the one to go. And then I would be yet another person gone, making Nissa feel even more abandoned.

I remembered her arms around me, the emotions we'd shared, and knew I couldn't do it. Not yet.

And truth be told, I wasn't ready to leave Damian, either. Though I'd known him only for a few days, I was drawn to him like no other man.

He was pacing now. "What happened to Dawn, then? Did someone get rid of her?" He stared at me and shook his head. "The things that have been happening to you… What if they weren't accidents?"

"There are some pretty strange things going on here, all right," I agreed.

What if they *weren't* accidents? What if someone really wanted me dead?

"Priscilla!" Damian wrenched out. "Is it possible she could be doing these things? If she was here tonight, without my knowing, then anything is possible."

He was talking more to himself than to me. His agitation was contagious. But I didn't even know Priscilla. What could she have against me?

"So you do think Nissa saw her mother?"

"I'm afraid so." He ran a hand through his hair. "My ex-wife has practically bankrupted the farm with her demands of money. She made herself quite a deal…she knows she's not welcome on the property, but apparently she can't stay away even if she's the one who left us."

So I'd been correct that Priscilla's not being around was to Damian's liking. But I wondered what he meant by her making a deal. And why would she be sneaking around?

I asked, "If she didn't come here to see her daughter…then why?"

"I imagine she's the one who has been rummaging around in the attic. No doubt I can thank Mrs. Avery for letting her in. And for covering for her."

"You think she's been searching for the Equine Diamonds?"

"Nothing would surprise me where Priscilla is concerned. She's a liar and a cheat. You can't trust anything she tells you."

A liar and a cheat. I swallowed hard. Damian could be describing me.

"My ex-wife could never have enough of anything,"

he went on. "She ran through money like water, but over the past several months she's had her lawyers hounding me for more. Apparently she made some bad investments. She's been playing me, suggesting that I wouldn't want to see the mother of my child out on the streets."

"I...I'm sure that wasn't your intention."

"Of course not. I mortgaged this place to give her enough money in the divorce settlement to satisfy her. The money could have supported her for a decade. Maybe now you see why I say not seeing her mother is best for Nissa. Priscilla has destroyed her own life. I don't want her to ruin Nissa's, as well. I *won't* let that happen. My daughter is the most important thing in the world to me."

Damian's emotions were raw and on the surface. I was deeply moved by his love and protectiveness for Nissa, something I had longed for myself once my father had taken himself out of my life for good. My foster parents had been kind, caring people, but I'd never been able to forget what I'd lost.

Damian's concern and, yes, his obvious pain over the situation, made me feel closer to him, opened up my heart to him. I sensed he felt his world was crumbling, one brick and then another. I knew how devastating that could be, and I wanted to help him hold on.

For the second time in one evening, I wrapped comforting arms around another human being. First the daughter, now the father.

Strong arms wrapped around my back and pulled me closer in response. "Ah, Chloe..." He murmured my name, his lips pressed against my hair.

And then his lips inched from my temple to my cheek with aching slowness. Slowness meant, no doubt, to give me time to move away. Such slowness that I found it hard to breathe when I didn't.

I gasped as his mouth slid over mine.

Damian kissed me with such thoroughness that the effect traveled along every nerve, all the way to my toes. I gave as good as I got and I knew that I had never felt so sweetly ravaged or so thoroughly seduced just from a kiss.

His forehead pressed to mine, Damian murmured, "Chloe, maybe you should go back to the house."

"Is that what you want? For me to go?"

"No."

"Then don't send me away."

I wrapped my arms around the back of his neck and tugged until our mouths meshed once more.

Damian groaned and turned me until my back was pressed up against a stall wall. His hands skimmed my sides—waist to breasts, breasts to thighs. His fingers curled in the material of my skirt and he inched it upward. Sensation ran down my thighs and up to my center. A wet warmth pooled there in anticipation of his more intimate touch.

When his fingertips skimmed my thighs, I moaned into his mouth and spread my legs for him. No need for further invitation. Bold fingers slid along my panties, now damp with my growing desire. He hooked the elastic and found the swollen wet center. One touch and my mind began to float…my heart began to pound…my body began to tremble….

I needed this. I'd needed it for so long. Not simply the promise of sexual satisfaction, but a deeper meeting, a total connection with someone who validated everything I'd yearned for in my life.

"Damian!" I cried as he touched my center and I felt my universe begin to shift.

He answered with another kiss, his tongue plunging into my mouth, his finger plunging into my body. I quaked and clung to him and felt my mind shatter.

He held me until I floated back down and my heart settled into a steady beat.

And then he pulled back, took my hand and led me into the stall. We kissed again, and I wanted to give him the same pleasure he'd given to me.

The thought that someone had gotten rid of Dawn and now wanted to do the same to me drifted at the back of my mind.

If I didn't make love to him the way I wanted to now, I might not have another chance….

I attacked his zipper with trembling fingers. My legs were like rubber and I stumbled into him. He fell back against the hay bale, bringing me with him on top of the blanket. I could feel him hard and ready for me against my inner thigh. He tugged at my panties and freed me of them, then pulled me over him. As I straddled him, I heard the crinkle of foil and knew he was putting on a condom. When he was ready, I sank down his length with agonizing slowness.

His groan inflamed me. I held his hot gaze, and as I began slowly rocking over him, I unbuttoned my blouse. His gaze touched my breasts…followed by his hands.

He thumbed me through the lace-trimmed material of my bra until my nipples stood out in hard peaks. Then one hand slid down where we were joined together, his fingers slipping against my center.

"Now," he whispered, urging me with his hips.

I rode him deeply and wildly as if this were the only time we would be together like this.

As indeed it might be….

When I came this time, it was like riding out a storm—thunder and lightning and pelting rain. And in the midst of my climax, Damian shuddered inside me. We panted in unison and stared at each other for an interminable moment as if to ask, What now?

Then Damian pulled me to his side, where he held me as if he would never let me go.

Chapter Fourteen

Only after I slept for several hours did I wake wondering what I had been thinking in becoming intimate with my employer.

I looked down at Damian, softly snoring, and my heart did a dance. He was so darkly handsome that it nearly hurt to look at him, but look I did—at the thick lashes brushing his cheeks, the bared chest and arms roped with muscle from hard work, the narrow waist, muscular thighs and the part of him that had brought me most pleasure. Even now he seemed nearly ready to please me yet again.

Before that could happen, before I talked myself into believing there could be something lasting between us, I slipped from his side, gathered my clothes flung around the hay bales, and put them on as fast as I was able to manage.

What would a man like Damian Graylord want with his daughter's tutor?

I was about to slip away unnoticed when I realized he was awake and watching me through slitted eyes.

"Why such a hurry to get away, Chloe?"

"It's almost morning."

"Were you planning on just leaving me?"

The words echoed hollowly through my head, and I almost believed they had a deeper significance than my trading the barn for the house.

I shook the thought away.

"I was just going to my room." After all, now that my head had cleared of the lust he'd instigated, I didn't want to fool myself into thinking there would be more than sex between us. At least, not on his part. "You were sleeping."

"I'm not sleeping now, so the least you could do is kiss me good morning."

My knees threatened to give way, but I steeled myself and backed toward the stall opening. "I wouldn't want to give you any ideas."

"I have ideas enough already."

I could see that he did.

Making a choked sound, I fled the stall and swore I heard laughter follow me out of the barn. Damian laughing? Would the surprises never end?

So why wasn't I enjoying them? Why did I want to run? Part of me felt like getting in my car and driving and never looking back. I could take with me a few sweet memories of Damian and Nissa, with them still believing in me.

But what about Dawn?

Perhaps my friend had staged her own disappearance to cover up her connection to Centaur's death. But what if she hadn't? What if the truth was more complicated than that? I knew I had to finish what I'd started and ferret out the truth.

Crossing the yard to the house, I felt as if hidden eyes followed. Priscilla's? Was she still here? Or someone more dangerous? My pulse twitched and my breath grew shallow and my ears seemed to ring with panic. I hurried, watching for any threat, but I noted nothing out of place as I let myself in the back door and rushed up the stairs.

By the time I got to the second floor, I was calmer. I was also aware of a scratchy discomfort at the base of my neck. As I reached my door, I pulled out a handful of straw from the back of my blouse—a reminder of what I'd been doing with Damian. The fresh hay scent made me smile.

Then another door clicked open and a faint voice called out, "Mama?"

I jerked around to see a pajama-clad Nissa standing outside her door. As she focused on me—on what was in my hand—her forehead pulled into a frown.

Then her accusing gaze met mine. "You were in the barn with Dad? All night?"

"Nissa—"

She flew into her room and slammed the door behind her. I was torn about going to her. Explanations might be better left unmade.

Besides, what was I supposed to tell her? Certain that she'd guessed her father and I had done more than just talk, I was equally certain she hated the idea. Kids always hoped their estranged parents would get back together, and she'd seen her mother on the grounds. No doubt Nissa's had been the eyes I'd felt watching me come from the barn. No doubt she had hoped it was Priscilla.

My mood plummeting, I retreated to my bedroom. I

didn't want to hurt Nissa. She'd experienced enough emotional trauma over the past year. It wouldn't be fair to make her suffer over my night of passion, one that I would make certain wasn't repeated. Damian and I had no future, and there was no sense in acting as though we did. I wondered if I could pretend that nothing had happened—that I hadn't fallen for Damian Graylord—and fool Nissa into believing that.

One glance in the mirror told me I'd already betrayed myself to the girl. My hair was a tousled mess with bits of hay sticking out all over. In my haste to leave the barn, I'd misbuttoned my blouse. And the reddish splotch on my neck was a definite giveaway.

What kind of disaster had I wreaked?

AS THE MORNING PROGRESSED Damian's mood quickly turned foul. First Theo called in saying he had a family emergency and wouldn't be in until sometime that afternoon. Then he'd realized his brother had done a disappearing act. Alex had driven off right after dinner the night before and hadn't so much as called in to say where he was or what time he was planning on getting back. Clifford had shown up—surly as usual—and was mucking the stalls.

Everything else was in Damian's lap, and he'd had to take time out to talk to the deputy who'd finally come around to take stock of the feed theft.

All the while he was working, his mind buzzed off and on with the women in his life. Memories of Chloe's softness and warmth were overshadowed by his exasperation with his ex-wife, who was invading his space at the least, responsible for the attacks on Chloe at the worst.

When had Priscilla changed? he wondered. Or had she really? Perhaps he'd been so enamored of her sexual allure when he'd met her that he'd been blinded to the truth of her nature. Well, he'd quickly learned what she was—a coldhearted liar and a cheat. All that sex appeal had been, and was still, part of her facade. Nothing he'd believed about her had been genuine. As skilled as she'd been in bed, he'd never once felt with her what he'd felt with the less-experienced Chloe the night before on that simple bed of hay.

Chloe… Thinking about her calmed him down so he could get some work done. Thinking about her made him smile. Thinking about her made him believe there was some hope for his future.

He kept remembering her responses to him—genuine, without artifice. Each time she'd climaxed, she'd seemed genuinely surprised. He was getting hard just thinking about it. About her. About them together.

He decided if he wanted to get his work done, he'd better stay away from the young woman who obsessed his thoughts and his body, so he had Mrs. Avery deliver his lunch to the barn office. Eating there would allow him to keep an eye on the mare whose foal was overdue. He'd give her one more night, and then he'd call the vet to check on her, just in case she was the latest victim of the farm's bad-luck cycle.

The housekeeper came with his lunch on a tray that she set on his desk. There was a generous bowl of Merle's warmed-up chili, a couple of thick slices of bread, a mug of coffee and a couple of fat chocolate-chip cookies.

"Will that be all, Mr. Damian?"

"For lunch? That'll do it."

The housekeeper nodded and started to leave.

"One moment, Mrs. Avery."

She turned back to him, her eyebrows raised question marks.

Damian kept his tone casual when he said, "About Priscilla…how is she?"

"Why, however would I know?"

"You keep in touch with her, don't you? When was the last time you saw her?" For a few seconds he saw the guilt in her expression before she covered.

"I'll have to think about that."

"I mean what time…*last night?*"

The housekeeper turned more ashen than usual. "I…I'm not certain I know what you mean, Mr. Damian."

"Let's not play games. I know my ex-wife was here last evening. Nissa saw her."

"Nissa is a child with a child's imagination."

"But Chloe isn't. So has Priscilla been the one in the attic searching for the Equine Diamonds? Or was that your nephew? Or perhaps Priscilla and Larson together?" He'd never discovered the identity of his ex-wife's lover, but Jack Larson fit the bill in more ways than one.

The housekeeper drew herself up stiff and straight as if she had a steel rod for a spine. Her lips were pursed in disapproval, as if she was trying to appear formidable. Intimidating, even. But Damian was in no mood to humor her.

"I hope Priscilla or your nephew is willing to take you in, Mrs. Avery, because if I catch either one of them in my house or on my property without my knowledge again, you will no longer be employed by Graylord Pastures. Is that clear?"

"Yes, sir," she said stiffly. "But if I may...I never let either of them into the house."

"Semantics. You knew they were there, and—"

"Not 'they.' Your wife."

Now he was getting somewhere. "I am no longer married to Priscilla, Mrs. Avery. You know that. You also know she's been searching for those cursed diamonds in the attic. That's why you locked the door—so no one could accidentally stumble in on her. And you stood guard while she was up there." Her not denying it was as good as an admission. "That'll be all, then."

He followed her out of the office and watched her walk the length of the barn without looking back once. He might pay her salary, but it was obvious her loyalties still lay with his ex-wife. Even if she never let Priscilla into the house again, he should replace the housekeeper. At the moment the task seemed daunting. And how could he pull someone new into the household when he didn't know how long he would be able to pay her?

He settled down to his lunch and ate in record time. He checked on the mare again—she was getting restless—then went back into the office to call Priscilla for the third time that day. Yet again he got her voice mail.

"Priscilla—dammit, return my call! I want to know what the hell you think you're doing, sneaking around here and upsetting Nissa. We had a deal written in stone!

I paid you well to stay away for good, and I expect you to abide by the terms of the contract!"

A rustling behind him warned him he wasn't alone. Damian flipped around to find Chloe standing in the doorway, her great gray eyes wider than he'd ever seen them. She'd overheard his message. This was the moment he'd dreaded—her learning the truth about his divorce.

"You actually paid your ex-wife to stay away?" she asked, sounding shocked.

"I did it for Nissa." His words were as stiff as his stance. "Priscilla wanted the money more than she wanted her own child."

"Then she should have been able to learn her mother's true nature for herself." Chloe's eyes pleaded with him, but she kept her distance. "That doesn't mean Nissa would have rejected her…or been like her. She's her own person and she has you to guide her."

The moment he'd seen Chloe, he'd wanted to take her in his arms and lose himself as he had last night, but his ardor was cooling. "Our life would have been hell with Priscilla in it."

"You mean *your* life would have been hell."

"My life was already hell. Isn't fourteen years a long enough sentence for allowing myself to be charmed by the wrong woman?"

"You didn't have to stay married to her all those years. You didn't even have to see her just because your daughter did. Mrs. Avery could take Nissa to see her mother."

"I suppose she could," Damian said, unable to stop the chill from entering his voice.

Indeed, that had been an option, but he'd known that

Nissa would have felt her loyalties ripped in two. She would have been caught in the middle between feuding parents forever. He hadn't wanted a lifetime of strife for her. He'd truly thought that once Priscilla was out of her life for good, she would adjust and find happiness.

"It's not too late to admit you made a mistake," Chloe said.

"I did make a mistake fourteen years ago. Nissa was the only good thing to come of it."

Chloe's expression was sad. He could feel her disappointment in him. So why did that make him feel worse than he already did?

"I'm looking for Nissa," she said, her tone now sounding distant. "Has she been to see you?"

"No. Why? Is something wrong?"

"Nissa saw me coming from the barn this morning. Apparently, she thought I was Priscilla until we had a face-to-face in the hall. She's angry with me. She ate breakfast in silence. I couldn't get her interested in a lesson, not even using horses."

Damian clenched his jaw. That kind of behavior reminded him of his ex-wife. "I'll speak to her."

"Your talking to Nissa would be good—just not about me. I need to speak to her myself."

"She's my—"

"Daughter," Chloe finished for him. "Yes, I know. You've reminded me often enough. But you can't fix it this time, Damian."

Gearing up to tell her that he could and he would, Damian heard Clifford yelling, but couldn't make out the problem.

"What's that about?" he muttered, moving to the nearest window to find out.

The sight before him almost made his heart stop—his beloved child was in danger.

I COULD HARDLY BELIEVE IT when Damian shoved by me to get out the door.

"What is it?" I asked.

"Nissa!"

My pulse speeding as fast as my feet, I followed him through the barn and out the back door. My heart nearly stopped when I saw the cause of his concern.

Clifford was in the pasture, ineffectively trying to stop Nissa, who was riding what had to be the biggest, most powerful stallion on the farm. She wasn't relaxed and sure of herself as she had been on Wild Cherry, and I could see her tension wiring straight to the horse. He threw up his great neck and changed the cadence of his trot. His legs were stiffer and pumping faster.

"Nissa, stay calm and bring Satan's Dance over here," Damian said in a steady voice. "You can do it, honey."

I stopped at the fence, while he climbed over it and headed straight for her. I wanted to do more than watch, but I didn't know what I could do. My efforts would undoubtedly distract Damian, so I stayed put.

Either Nissa was ignoring her father or she was having so much trouble with the stallion that she wasn't hearing him. Satan's Dance was gathering himself up—his muscles were bunching, his dark bay hide shone with sweat, and if the foam around his mouth were any indication, he was working the bit.

"Oh, Nissa..."

This was her way of striking back at the people who'd disappointed her. This was the Nissa that I hadn't seen since that first introduction. She was angry and she was scared and she was taking it out on herself.

Please don't get hurt....

I gripped the fence board tightly and watched the dance between stallion, girl and men. Damian moved quickly and smoothly straight-on, while Clifford circled behind horse and rider. Nissa was trying her best to collect the stallion, but he was having none of it. The closer the men got, the more agitated he became, until with a shrill shriek, he lowered his head and triggered.

Talk about a car going zero to sixty in six seconds being impressive, when the vehicle was flesh and bone, zero to thirty—and I swore that's what Satan's Dance was doing—was astounding. My heart in my throat, I watched Nissa, frightened but determined, body stretched low over the massive neck, her fingers tightly gripping the reins, as the horse flew around the pasture. Both men froze to the spot, and like me, I'm sure, prayed the horse wouldn't stumble or startle, which he could do at any sudden movement. I prayed that Nissa could just hang on. Satan's Dance couldn't keep up this pace forever.

Damian was rooted, turning, his gaze fixed on his daughter, his muscles bunched just like the horse. His fear for her consumed me. I couldn't catch my breath.

On his second course around the pasture, the horse began to tire and slow. Nissa let up her death grip on the reins, and her body appeared fluid again. I watched her hands and legs as she attempted to collect the horse. The struggle was short-lived. The horse slowed, then stopped short with one last twist of defiance.

And Nissa pitched forward over his shoulder and landed flat on her back on the ground.

"Nissa!" I yelled, climbing over the fence to get to her, fearing a head or neck injury since she hadn't worn her hat.

Damian got there first, but when he tried to touch his daughter, she pushed him away and got to her feet on her own.

"I'm all right! Leave me alone!" Nissa yelled.

Relieved, I slowed and stayed where I was. She was angry with me, after all.

Clifford clucked and shook his head and went after Satan's Dance, who now stood calmly, as if he hadn't just caused hearts to stop.

"What were you thinking, young lady?"

"I just wanted to ride Satan's Dance," Nissa said, her expression sullen.

"You could have been injured or worse!"

"Nothing bad happened. I'm fine."

"Your *attitude* isn't fine," Damian told her. "It needs an immediate adjustment!"

Damian was yelling because he'd been terrified for her, I knew, but I could see it was the wrong approach. Nissa dug in her heels and wouldn't back down. Why, oh, why, couldn't he just put his arms around his daughter and tell her how much she meant to him?

Tell her he loved her and no matter what, that wouldn't change?

No matter what, he would never leave her?

That's really all she wanted.

That's really all *I'd* wanted....

"I'm not the one who is doing anything wrong," Nissa said, sliding a glance at me when she said that.

Guilt stabbed me, and once more I was finding it hard to breathe. In no way did I want to come between Nissa and Damian.

"*No one* is doing anything wrong," Damian said.

From his emphasis on no one, I gathered he was subtly telling her that we hadn't done anything wrong.

I wasn't so certain.

I backed away from the argument, more convinced than ever that—despite my feelings for him—getting intimate with Damian had been a mistake. How could I fix it? How could I make Nissa trust me again?

"I don't ever want you to do anything so foolish again."

Though I knew Damian was furious with his daughter, he sounded more than reasonable.

Not so Nissa.

"You keep calling me 'young lady.'" She crossed her arms and glared at him. "That means I'm not a child anymore. And I'll do what I want!"

"If you don't curb your behavior, come September, I will send you to that boarding school. Maybe the teachers there can teach you some discipline!"

Nissa's grown-up facade crumbled and with a cry, she ran from the pasture. Damian watched until she was headed toward the house. Then he looked at me and shook his head in disgust.

Remembering my father looking at me like that just before he'd left me, I felt chilled all the way through.

Chapter Fifteen

"Nissa, it's Chloe," I said after knocking at her door several hours later.

Nissa hadn't come down to eat, and I was worried about her. Damian had ignored her absence at the dinner table. Alex hadn't shown, either. Dinner had been a quiet affair, with me silently reevaluating Damian.

I tried again. "Nissa, honey?"

"Go away!"

Needing to know if she meant that literally, I said, "Is that what you really want, Nissa? For me to go away? Back to Chicago?"

Seconds later the door opened and Nissa stared out at me from the dark. The only light on in her room came from the fish tank. Even so, I could see enough to know that she was still upset.

"Can I come in?"

She shrugged her narrow shoulders and went back to her bed, where she threw herself on her stomach along the length of the mattress, as if she was intent on leaving me no room to sit near her.

So I stood.

"My heart nearly stopped today, Nissa. I was so afraid you were going to be hurt. Your dad was worried, too."

"I'm a good rider."

"But you don't ride stallions. You know you're not supposed to ride any horse other than Wild Cherry without your dad's permission."

"Dawn did. I saw her."

So that's what had gotten into her. Somehow she'd associated her anger for me with her feelings of abandonment by Dawn. A kid's mind was sometimes more complex than one might guess.

"I like it here, Nissa. I like *you.* I like tutoring you and I hope to keep doing so as planned until school starts. But if you really want me to go back to Chicago now, I need to know that."

"You're going to leave, too?"

Touched by her stricken tone, I shook my head. "Not if you don't want me to."

"Then don't," she said. "I'm sorry, okay?"

"Okay. I think your dad could stand to hear that, too."

Nissa didn't respond, and I didn't push it.

"So we're okay. We'll go back to our work schedule tomorrow."

"Uh-huh." She turned her head toward the wall.

The conversation was over.

Now I had to talk to Damian, which I expected would be even more difficult.

I found him in the library at his desk, staring at the computer monitor. I got him with his guard down. Just for a moment I could see how upset he was.

"What is it?" he asked, his guard back up.

"I just spoke to Nissa. She's still upset. I wanted to make sure it was all right with her that I stay."

"That's not her decision to make."

"It was *my* decision. I didn't want to make her more miserable than she was, Damian." I'd been willing to go—to give up on Dawn—for Nissa. But now that I meant to stay, I was going to fight for the girl. "Speaking of decisions, do you really mean to send her to a boarding school? That was the worst kind of threat to make to a child who already feels abandoned."

Damian stiffened. "Nissa has to know there are consequences to her actions."

"But not *that*."

"Look, I have my hands full trying to keep this farm going. I can't be continually worrying about Nissa and what she's gotten herself into because she's angry about something."

"Then get her counseling. Don't send her away."

"If I did, it would be for her own good. She is my daughter, and I'll decide her fate."

Just as my father had decided mine when he gave me up to the system. I wondered if he'd felt that was for my own good, too.

If hearing Damian admit to buying Priscilla off so she wouldn't try to see her child hadn't been enough, this did it for me. I simply couldn't have feelings for a man who would abandon his daughter to a boarding school.

Only, I did have feelings.

Part of me *wanted* to leave now, so that I could protect myself, but I would stay until summer's end for Nissa's sake.

And then I would never have to see Damian Graylord again.

THE TUTOR LEFT THE HOUSE, her skirts whipping around her in the rising wind. A storm was coming; the horses could sense it. They were restless and noisy. But Chloe seemed oblivious. She was turned into herself, seemingly unaware of her surroundings.

Unaware of the danger she'd put herself in.

Thanks to the Internet, the watcher knew who Chloe Morgan was and why she was there. Good thing when instincts were so well honed.

The teacher had motivated her eighth-grade class to do a documentary that had won a state prize. Plugging her name into a search engine had quickly produced the photo of her at the dinner honoring the project. She'd been sitting next to her best friend.

Dawn Reed.

Which explained all the snooping around.

Chloe hadn't believed the fabricated elopement note. Her bad luck.

Trying to scare her off hadn't worked.

Scare time was over. She should've taken the hint and hightailed it back to Chicago.

Now there was only one way left to deal with her.

How should she die? Should it look like an accident? Or that Damian was responsible?

All this pressure to keep on top of this situation was exhausting. Becoming a murderer hadn't been part of the plan. Unfortunately, it had been necessary—the only solution when things had started going wrong.

Third time had damn well better be the charm!

MY HEART HEAVY, I was drawn to find my elusive link to Dawn—the horse who must really be a ghost.

Had Centaur's special connection to Dawn really survived his death? I had to believe so. He'd led me straight to the place where I'd found the hair ornament I'd given Dawn. They'd starred together in my dreams.

What had they been trying to tell me?

Maybe the bluffs held some answers, even if they were ones I didn't want to know. I pushed that thought back to where I didn't have to face it and cut through the woods.

I hadn't been able to settle down after my disagreement with Damian, so I'd decided to do something that would make me feel better. The bluffs called me. After finding Dawn's hair clip there, I felt as if they held answers, if only I could focus properly. Whether I found what I was looking for or not, at least I was making an effort and, considering how down I was right now, that was something.

It would keep me from thinking about him. About how disappointed I was in him. About how much his attitude toward his daughter wounded *me.*

Deep in the forested area, I relied on my flashlight to get me through the maze of trees. A noise to my left startled me, leaving me with a heart beating double time.

I stopped at the familiar sounds whispering along the leaves. Was Centaur nearby, then? I closed my eyes and listened with a new intensity....

The sounds gradually define themselves...a soft whicker...a neigh...the thud of hooves against soft earth.

I whistle...call him in my mind....

"Centaur!"

The gray moves through the trees...great neck arching...mane flying...tail swishing....

My heart begins to drum in rhythm. I wait...wait...wait as the pale stallion draws closer and then stops.

He knows me now. No more weaving and bobbing and flying past me. He stands quietly in the mist and stares at me from liquid dark eyes. In silent appeal, he begs me...for what? I don't understand.

"What do you want me to know?" I ask as I open my eyes.

For the first time I saw him as he really was...magnificent head...long, strong legs rising from the fog-shrouded forest floor...powerful, *translucent* body...nothing but a pale shadow against the night. My flashlight beam cut straight through him to the trees beyond. It seemed to me that one good puff of wind and he would dissipate, his form no more solid than smoke.

He was real...and yet not.

I took a deep breath and waited to see what he required of me. The ghost horse snorted and bobbed his head and turned away. He took a few steps and glanced back as if to make sure I was following.

"I'm coming."

He whickered and moved off, his long stride easily switching from a comfortable walk to a trot. When the gap between us suddenly widened, my power walk quickly turned into a jog. My feet slapped against soft earth, stirring up the scent of decay as I ran. The rush of a racing river swept through me as surely as the blood in my veins. He was leading me straight for the palisades along the Mississippi.

Was he doomed to haunt them, then? Was this his lot forever?

Or was there something he needed—from me—to set him free?

Is that why he chose to appear to me and me alone?

I wished Damian were here to see him. Maybe he would understand what the stallion wanted. Then again, maybe not. Damian was a man who only understood what he deemed reasonable and logical and within his power to control.

Just when I thought I could run no farther, the stallion stopped and whinnied. He was in the clearing near the palisades. The sky was threatening. Thunderheads were rolling, hiding the clouds, but the moon avoided them and cast its blue gleam over the fog-draped bluffs.

Breathing hard, I slowed and only stopped when I got within yards of my guide. Ghostly fingers of mist curled around his slender legs and slipped around his barrel.

His translucent flesh trembled as he paced…circled…waited for me.

"What?" I asked. "What is it I'm supposed to see?"

He stopped and snorted and as if he exhaled a breeze, the fog before me rolled to the sides, revealing a narrow opening in the rocky outcropping that could be a trail of sorts.

How had I missed that before? I wondered.

I stepped to the path, and my guide backed, backed,

backed into a wall of fog until his image was consumed. Now my flashlight was my only guide.

Was this it, then?

Would this trail lead me to the answers I sought?

My pulse skittered along my veins and kick-started my descent. My light's narrow beam led me down and around in a serpentine path that crossed halfway under the bluff. Below, the river had been kicked up by the strong winds. The current was raging. Anything falling down into its depths would be swept away in an instant.

I looked up and realized the rocky overhang would keep anyone above from seeing this path, if one could even call it that. Barely a foot wide with brush and rock on either side, the crude track undulated and eventually circled back in toward the bluff.

That's where I saw the opening, half-hidden in a jagged crevice.

My heart began to thunder and my mouth went dry as I cautiously approached. I slid the beam all around the opening and noticed a pile of rocks to one side, as if someone had dug them free and tossed them there.

Rocks that had once blocked the entrance to a tunnel?

Damian had told me that he and Alex had been trapped in the tunnel that led from the house to the river, that rocks had blocked all but an opening too small for a child to crawl through. Had someone found the entrance and unblocked it? Someone who'd used the tunnel to get to the passageway and hidden staircase that led to the attic?

Wondering what this had to do with Centaur and Dawn, I knew there was only one way to find out.

The opening was narrow, but someone bigger than I—a man—could get through if he turned sideways. I slipped inside and waited until my eyes adjusted. Not that there was anything to see but walls and floor and ceiling of rock.

Following my flashlight beam, I edged my way through the yard-wide tunnel, floor strewn with loose rocks, wondering if any minute I would have a nasty surprise. A dozen yards in and the floor softened as did the walls. My flashlight revealed earth mixed with rock underfoot and wooden beams holding back the sides and top of the tunnel.

The space was eerie—dark and airless—and I could only guess the terror being trapped in here had caused Damian and his brother.

Loose gravel and small rocks trailed along the floor. As careful as I tried to be, I felt a surge of nerves and missed a beat. I stepped wrong, and my ankle twisted. I tried to catch myself but couldn't stop from pitching forward. My flashlight went spinning out of my hand, and I went down to the ground.

The air was knocked out of me for a moment, but when I was able to take a deep breath, I nearly gagged. A foul odor filled the chamber. I held my breath. On hands and knees, I reached for the flashlight, praying that it hadn't been damaged and that it wouldn't go out. I felt a bit better once it was safely in my hand and the beam didn't waver.

I pulled back and swept the beam across a nearby pile of rocks. Something pale amidst them caught my eye.

I tugged at a rock. It came away easily as did the

next and the next after that. Suddenly, something slid toward me.

I screamed.

The smell…

A human hand….

Bloated as it was, I could still see the tattoo around the wrist—the same Celtic design mirrored in the hair ornament.

"No! Please no!" I sobbed, my heart breaking at the truth I'd been trying to deny.

At last I'd found Dawn.

Dead….

Chapter Sixteen

Damian sat on the edge of Nissa's bed and listened to her even breathing for a while. He used to do this nightly when she was a little girl, before he'd gotten too busy trying to keep her mother satisfied. Everything he'd done, he'd done for Nissa. Married Priscilla. Stayed with the grasping cheat for years when he didn't have to. Then paid her off to give Nissa some peace in her innocent life.

And Chloe Morgan probably despised him for the last.

Perhaps her opinion shouldn't be so important to him, but it was. He'd known her for barely a week and he felt closer to her than to the woman who'd been his wife for more than a dozen years. Chloe was the kind of woman he'd wished for as a mother to his children.

Kind…patient…loving.

Mostly the loving part. And he didn't just think of the sex. She'd comforted him when he'd needed it most, just as she had his child. He wanted to feel her arms around him again. He wanted to surround her with himself and know that at last fate had looked kindly at him. And at his daughter.

He stroked a strand of hair from Nissa's face and bent over to kiss her forehead. Her sigh made his chest squeeze tight.

Amazingly similar to the way he'd felt when Chloe had walked out on him earlier.

She'd been right about his not sending Nissa to a boarding school. He'd been exasperated, worried to death and obviously not in his right mind. Life wouldn't be worth living if his daughter weren't in it every day. It was just that sometimes he didn't know how to handle a thirteen-year-old girl with issues.

He would have to learn.

Rising, he pulled the coverlet up to Nissa's shoulders, and before leaving the room, he lowered her window. Thunder rumbled in the distance. Another storm was brewing.

One last look at his sleeping daughter and he crossed the bedroom, quietly closing the door behind him.

He needed to check on the still-pregnant mare. The vet had reassured him the foal was fine—it was just taking its time. Theo was with the mare tonight, but Damian wouldn't rest easy until he checked on her for himself.

But first he needed to see Chloe.

He needed to talk to her, to come to some understanding. Nissa needed her. *He* needed her. He feared that, like Dawn, she might just vanish in the middle of the night, never to be seen again. Dawn's leaving had made him grieve for his daughter's sake. Chloe's doing the same would make him grieve for them both.

And, indeed, when knocking at her door didn't get a response, he dreaded having lost her already.

"Chloe?" he called.

Nothing.

As much as he hated invading anyone's privacy, he wanted to make sure she was all right. He opened her door and looked inside, but she wasn't there. Her things were, however—her laptop, a pair of shoes discarded beside a chair and a nightgown across her bed. She hadn't gone.

Yet.

Worried now—had something *else* untoward happened to her?—he closed the door and started for the back stairs when he realized Mrs. Avery was watching him from her doorway. Was Priscilla in the house, then? Did the housekeeper fear that he would find his ex-wife in the attic?

"Is there something I can do for you, Mr. Damian?"

"Where's Priscilla?"

"I…I wouldn't know."

"Don't lie!"

"I haven't heard from her since yesterday. I swear. To tell you the truth, I'm a bit worried—"

He cut her off with *"Where is Chloe?"* and tried to read her for any sign of guilt.

Thunder rumbled ominously in the distance as Mrs. Avery grew tight-lipped. "Last I saw, Chloe was going for another of her evening strolls."

Damian cursed under his breath. "Not into the woods?"

"I'm sure I wouldn't know, sir."

But *he* did.

Rushing down the stairs, he grabbed a flashlight before heading out into the night, already damp with the threatened rain. He was trying not to panic, but he couldn't help himself. That Priscilla wasn't beyond trying to scare Chloe away didn't escape him. He didn't think she was capable of killing anyone, but then, he'd been wrong about her before. Or what if he'd been right about Larson being his ex-wife's lover. He didn't know what Larson might be willing to do for her.

So Chloe could be a target yet again.

Why in the world would she go out for a walk alone at night after all the things that had been happening to her?

He wanted to throttle her.

Wanted to hold her in his arms.

Wanted to make sure she was safe forever.

I SAT CURLED IN A BALL against the wall opposite Dawn's grave and tried not to breathe in the fetid smell of her rotting body. I rocked and moaned for who knew how long.

I wanted to cry…tried to cry…couldn't.

Why was I unable to express my grief?

Maybe because, all along, I'd known. Dawn would never abandon me. How many times had I told myself that?

I'd known…I'd known!

Now that I was faced with the reality, I couldn't pretend anymore. I couldn't fabricate stories like Dawn taking off because she'd felt guilt over Centaur's death. She'd had nothing to do with it….

Or had she?

A chill shot through me as I realized the stallion's death might not have been an accident.

What if she'd been a witness?

What if Centaur hadn't accidentally run off the cliff? What if it had been murder? First the horse, then my friend…

Could Priscilla have done this?

No one had a good word to say about the woman. She'd practically bankrupted the farm and had wanted more money that Damian didn't have. Wanted the Equine Diamonds enough to sneak around behind Damian's back.

What if she'd wanted more?

Her daughter…Damian…the farm itself.

The last made me think of Jack Larson. *He* wanted the farm. *He* was Mrs. Avery's nephew.

What if they were in it together, all three of them?

How evil did a person have to be that he would do anything to get what he wanted?

How evil, to drive a stallion off a bluff to help bring financial ruin to Graylord Pastures?

How evil, to kill someone simply because she'd witnessed what she shouldn't?

The questions were there, but the truth was too horrible to fathom. I wanted different answers. A different suspect. Someone other than Priscilla.

I didn't want Nissa to be destroyed by the truth about her mother.

Above that, I didn't want to die.

"Dawn, I'm so sorry. I have to leave you for now," I whispered as though she could hear me. "But I'll tell them where to find you. There has to be evidence on you. Fibers. Something. They'll figure out who did this to you."

I wanted to touch her hand, but I couldn't. That wasn't Dawn anymore. Dawn was… I was going to say *in a better place,* but was she?

Or was she trapped here like Centaur, a phantom doomed to walk the earth until justice was served in her behalf?

I backed away, toward the mouth of the tunnel. The winds had picked up, the sound like a warning cry whipping around the entrance and echoing around me.

I had to get to Damian. He would know what to do. He would help me see that justice was done.

A few steps in the right direction and the tainted air dissipated. I could breathe normally again. Or as normally as a person could after finding the body of someone they loved. I'd lost them all now—mother, father, foster sister…all my family.

And when Damian knew the truth about me—that I'd been lying about my intentions all along—I would lose him, too. And Nissa. Another reason to grieve, for it had become clear to me that I loved them both.

I tried not to think of anything but getting to safety as I escaped the tunnel. A thick blanket of fog had rolled up from the river, blinding me as effectively as the dark itself. My flashlight was practically useless—I couldn't even see my own feet. So I slid them, one at a time, keeping shoe contact with the ground, staying on the twisting path by memory and feel rather than by sight. Every so often a gust of wind threatened to knock me over.

One wrong step and it would all be over….

I was practically to the top of the bluff, if my instincts

were right, when what sounded like a foghorn blasted toward me, startling me into stepping wrong.

"Ahhh!"

My feet slid back and I teetered, ending my awkward balancing act by throwing myself forward. My hands smacked into the rock wall. My flashlight wavered but thankfully didn't go out. It took me a moment to catch my breath.

Nothing unusual about a foghorn on the river in this weather…but the sound had been so close. Weird.

My pulse steadied and I got my feet under me and began moving again.

Only, something didn't feel right. Call it instinct or premonition or whatever, but I sensed I wasn't alone. Another blast of sound convinced me, because it wasn't coming from the river, but somewhere overhead…as if someone was trying to scare me into falling.

My pulse raced and my stomach knotted and my instincts went on alert. Sensing trouble, I clicked off my flashlight, slipped it into my pocket and took slow, quiet breaths. Someone had killed my best friend and now I feared that same someone—Priscilla?—was waiting to do the same to me.

What choice did I have? If I went back into the tunnel, I would be trapped, a sitting duck for a murderer. There was no other way down—no other path to take. So up I would go—at least once I got to the top of the bluff, I would have a chance to escape.

A third blast of the horn jangled my nerves, but I kept my head. Setting off again, moving cautiously, I tried not to make any noise. My senses were on alert for any hint of movement above.

Nothing….

Any scuffle.

Nothing….

Any breath.

Nothing….

At least not until my hands went wild feeling for the rock face, which suddenly disappeared. Off balance, I caught myself from falling forward. I'd reached the top of the bluff. That's when I heard a skitter of gravel to my left. *A footstep.* And a gust of wind cleared the fog just enough that I saw a dark silhouette. I stopped holding back and ran for all I was worth. Feet slapped behind me, followed by the sound of sliding gravel and a low-throated curse.

Another burst of speed shot me out of the fog, across the clearing toward the woods. I didn't stop to look for my pursuer. For all I knew, the person could be right behind me; blood rushing through my head had cut off other sounds, and my vision narrowed until my focus was the path directly in front of me. I ran fast and hard until, limbs quaking, chest heaving, I slowed and took a good look around.

The trees had thinned here and I spotted house lights through the thicket. The wind rattled branches above me, ratcheting up my nerves. I thought I would be closer, but I feared that in my wild flight, I had looped around to the other side of the clearing.

I stopped just for a moment to catch my breath and pull my flashlight from my pocket so I could see my way home. Thunder rumbled closer now, followed by streaks of lightning that made the woods glow eerily. Gusts of wind made the trees sway like slowly moving behemoths groaning warnings.

I switched on my flashlight and started picking my way forward. I hadn't gone far when I spotted something on the ground that made my nerves stand on end.

Cautiously I shone the beam along the woman's body. Even before I noted the hair that lay in a tousled riot of dark red curls so much like Nissa's—even before another streak of lightning infused the nightmare scene with a ghastly glow—I suspected the woman's identity.

Priscilla Graylord was dead.

Once more I felt faint, and when I heard, "Chloe, where are you?" I yelled, "Damian!" and ran toward the voice.

Damian...Damian will keep me safe....

No matter that just an hour ago, I'd decided there could be nothing between us, I believed that Damian was a man I could count on.

A moment later, my panic nearly choking me, I broke into the clearing before the palisades. My wanting to believe Damian would make things right warred with the bodies I had found. A killer was out here somewhere. Wind whistled down my shirt, making my flesh quake. How could anyone make that right? And the danger wasn't over....

"There you are, Chloe."

That voice...not Damian!

My heart thundered and my head went light as I realized my imagination had led me straight to my own end. Slowly I turned and faced the killer. Lightning flickered, revealing his identity, making me gasp.

"That's right, easy now," he murmured, as if talking to one of the horses. "No sudden moves."

"You—"

"Killed your friend, Dawn? I'm afraid so. And now I'm going to have to kill you, too."

Theo Bosch, barn manager, stood before me, a gun aimed at my middle. Apparently, he'd discarded the foghorn for a more effective weapon.

I tried to pull my wits about me. Hoping to figure out some way out of this, I stalled for time.

"The least you could do is tell me *why* before I die, Theo."

"Simple. I wanted to take back what was mine."

"Bosch Barns? You killed two women and a stallion over a piece of property?"

Theo barked a bitter laugh. "Not quite that simple. Damian Graylord *deserves* to be destroyed. His stealing Bosch Barns from me was a start. Before that he took my woman."

"Your woman?"

"Priscilla. She was mine until she met Damian. He dazzled her with his wealth and promises of the good life. Before I even knew what was what, she eloped with him. When Damian bought out Bosch Barns, he had everything that should be mine. That's why I took the job here. Keep your friends close, your enemies closer," he muttered.

I realized his hatred of Damian had been brewing and building for years. If he'd been any kind of man in the past, hate born of jealousy had destroyed him.

"Damian knew that you and Priscilla—"

"Of course she didn't tell him!" Theo said impatiently. "She wasn't about to ruin a sweet deal. Priscilla was all for sweet deals, and as mistress of Graylord Pastures, she thought she'd hit candy land. She tried to send me away, but I knew it was just a matter of time before she turned on the man she'd married, because she didn't love him. And I was right. Damian was working hard, and Priscilla got bored. Restless. That's where I came in."

Theo was holding a gun steady on me, not seeming a bit nervous at the thought of killing again. I wouldn't go without a fight, but I had to admit my options were slim. I could either rush him and get shot for sure in the process or disappear back into the fog with nowhere to go but the tunnel, where I would be trapped.

Then again, option two would let me get my hands on a rock to use as a makeshift weapon. Not as effective as a gun perhaps, but it would have to do.

"Damian knew Priscilla was cheating on him and tried to make her the faithful wife," Theo was saying. "It worked for a while, but Priscilla grew more and more restless. She put her energies into buying expensive horses the farm couldn't afford. Eventually Damian cut her off from spending another cent. That did it for her. It didn't take her long to abandon him and the brat."

"And Damian mortgaged the estate to give her the divorce settlement she wanted," Chloe said.

"What she *wanted* was the estate and a life with me. I was going to get it for us. No one ever guessed I was the one behind all the things going wrong on the farm.

I knew every step Damian was going to make before he made it. I figured once we had our hands on the Equine Diamonds, that would be enough to buy this place."

His face had taken on a fanatic expression, and he sounded delusional. He was insane on some level. Had to be or he never would have done such terrible deeds.

Knowing I had to make my move soon, I said, "Damian will never sell."

"He'll be *forced* to sell!" Theo said indignantly. "A matter of time, is all."

"So Priscilla found the diamonds?" I asked, wanting to confirm it had been Damian's ex-wife in the attic.

"No, but *I* will."

So Priscilla had been in the house, had probably been the one to push me in the dark. "The chimney...was that an accident?"

"Not any more than your almost being run over in Galena." He sounded angry when he asked, "Why couldn't you take the hint and get out while you still could?"

Angry because he really didn't want to kill me? If so, then maybe I still had a chance.

"There's something I don't understand, Theo," I said, trying to make my voice sympathetic. "If you did all of this for Priscilla, how did she end up dead?"

Another lightning strike revealed the emotions warring across his features and the fact that his hand was shaking. He might have done evil things, but he didn't seem to be comfortable in his own skin. He really had cared about Priscilla, and despite the fact that he'd killed her, she was still his weak spot.

"When I suggested we forget about the damn diamonds and the farm and just take off, start a new life together elsewhere, Priscilla laughed at me, told me she wouldn't spend her life with a man who had nothing!"

"After all you did for her?" I asked, again playing the sympathetic listener, all the while inching back toward the curtain of fog rising off the river.

"Priscilla turned out to be an unappreciative bitch!"

Theo was losing it now, and I was about to take my chances, when I caught a glimpse of movement in the copse of trees behind him. My pulse jumped and I was hard-pressed not to give away the other presence.

The barn manager went on. "We fought about leaving and she said things she shouldn't have.... The next thing I knew my hands were around her neck. I didn't mean to kill her. It was an accident!"

More movement. A silhouette separated from the trees. I forced my attention on the barn manager and asked, "Was Dawn an accident, too?"

"Your friend?" He shook his head and seemed oddly sorry when he said, "Too bad that Dawn saw me force that damn horse off the bluff! I had nothing against her, but I had to kill her to keep her quiet. Just as I'm going to have to kill you."

I sensed rather than saw the silhouette move forward and I soared with hope. An adrenaline spike flushed me with energy and purpose.

"What I don't understand is why you left Priscilla in the open when you were so careful to bury Dawn in the tunnel."

"I left Priscilla where she could be found so that

Damian would get nailed for her murder!" Theo yelled as the sky lit, revealing features crazed with emotion. "Everything *is* his fault!"

I turned to look over Theo's shoulder. "Did you get that, Damian?"

Theo laughed again and raised his arm and aimed the gun. "You're just trying to distract me, but it won't work. Damian's at the house with the brat!"

"Wrong, Theo!" Damian yelled as he rushed the barn manager from behind.

Chapter Seventeen

As he rammed Theo, a shot blasted from the handgun, and Damian knew the bullet just missed Chloe.

Theo recovered fast and swung around. Damian concentrated on relieving him of the weapon. He got both hands on Theo's arm and the gun itself. They struggled for it…danced around…four hands and arms entangled. Thinking fast, Damian freed his right hand and elbow-jabbed Theo in his shoulder. The other man's hand went slack for a second, and the gun flew from it and skittered along the ground.

Damian was vaguely aware of Chloe going after it, but he didn't dare look away from his opponent.

As strong and fit as he was, Theo with his broad, muscular body was more so. For every jab Damian delivered, he got one better in return. Theo was a desperate man, and Damian wouldn't put it past him to fight dirty and do something totally unexpected.

So Damian did it first. He rushed Theo, shoulder leading, and connected with the other man's chest just below his throat. Theo made a choking sound and they both went flying to the ground.

"Damian!"

Chloe's cry distracted him for a second—all it took for Theo to roll over and land on his chest and wrap strong fingers around his neck, tight as a vise. Damian's efforts to loosen the madman's grip failed.

"Stop it, Theo, or I'll shoot!" Chloe screamed.

Theo's effort to strangle him intensified until Damian started to see white jags of light in front of his eyes. A shot rang out and Theo jerked. His grip loosened just for a second, but that was all it took for a gasping Damian to buck with all his strength and unseat the other man. He looked for blood oozing from anywhere, but apparently Chloe had simply shot into the air to startle him.

Theo came at him, and Damian hauled off and shoved the heel of his hand into the man's nose.

Theo screamed in agony.

Blood spurted everywhere. Clutching his face, he rolled to the side, for the moment threatless.

Gun still in hand, Chloe rushed to Damian. "Are you all right?"

"Now I am," he said, wanting nothing more than to take her in his arms. "Watch where you put that gun, though."

"Sorry." She whipped it away from him.

As he got to his feet, Damian eyed Theo, who was hunched over nursing his nose. Then he checked Chloe over, taking comfort in at least being able to touch her.

"You're all right?"

She nodded. "Thanks to you."

He was reaching to take the gun from her when, with a yell, the barn manager flew to his feet and threw his bigger body against Damian's, jerking him past Chloe. The force was impossible to resist, and, wrapped in the killer's grasp, Damian stumbled backward.

"Damian, the bluff!" Chloe screamed as the fog met them with its wet kiss. "Sto-o-op!"

But Damian couldn't stop.

Their bodies cut into the fog, accelerating toward the cliff's edge. Suddenly Theo stopped, released him and shoved with all his might. Damian went flying backward. He threw out his arms, and by some miracle—and a gust of wind at his back—kept his balance and stopped within inches of falling to his death.

Just then, a horse's neigh cut across the expanse, the high-pitched sound querulous.

What the hell was a horse doing out here?

Theo didn't seem to hear. He was focused on Damian. "This is it for you now, Damian! You're going over if I have to go with you!"

But a lightning strike accompanied by another neigh—this one with a bugling ring—flipped Theo around looking for its source. Damian quickly moved away from the bluff edge toward Chloe even as a puff of fog turned into a gray horse. It reared on hind legs and flashed its hooves at the barn manager.

Recognizing the conformation, the way the mane dipped over the stallion's forehead, Damian swore softly under his breath. "Centaur…"

"No! It can't be!" Theo yelled. "You're dead!"

The stallion's screeched neigh cut through the fog as it headed straight for Theo, who backed up, misstepped, then flapped his arms to stay balanced.

The gray reared again, and Damian could only hold on to Chloe and watch.

Theo scrambled for footing on solid ground as the gray ghost sideswiped him. The man's head plunged backward, his body following in a bizarre slow motion dance in midair. For a moment Theo seemed suspended, limbs flashing and twisting as he tried to catch himself.

And then he plummeted backward, headfirst, into the fog….

I GASPED AND HELD my ears against Theo's scream that stopped only when his body thudded against the rocks below.

Damian held me pressed against him but I was too numb to do more than register that I wasn't going to die just yet. My heart settled into something akin to a normal rhythm, and I searched the fog for the ghost horse.

When I didn't see him, I closed my eyes….

There he is, wreathed in tendrils of fog, his gray head turning, his liquid dark eyes searching for someone.

"I'm here," I say. "I know everything now. And you have your justice."

The stallion snorts and bobs and I sense another presence slip out of the mists. Her hair is golden and her face is still beautiful and her hands aren't bloated with death.

This is the way I remember Dawn.

She smiles at me and I feel from her both sadness and more. Hope. I feel hope….

Grabbing the stallion's mane, she throws herself up onto his back. He snorts and nickers and begins to back up.

"Goodbye, Dawn," I say, as she raises a hand and waves at me. Then horse and rider dissolve back into the mists....

"Chloe, are you all right?"

I blinked up into Damian's worried face. The worry was something that I felt more than was able to see in the dark, since the lightning had heralded a steady, driving rain.

"I'm as good as can be expected." I swallowed hard. "I found Dawn." Tears began to roll down my cheeks. "She's dead, Damian, she's dead."

Damian held me then, and I sobbed against his chest. Finally I could grieve for my friend who was lost to me forever.

Not forever....

The words formed in my mind and I realized that I still had memories and dreams and perhaps a distant future when I would see her again. For now, at least, Dawn's spirit was released from being trapped here by her murder. She and Centaur could ride out of the mists and into the sun.

And I could go home to Chicago.

THE ODD THING WAS that Damian didn't ask me about Dawn. He didn't ask if or how I knew her. He didn't ask. He simply listened as I told him about following the horse and finding the entrance to the tunnel and the horror inside.

Then he said we needed to call the authorities and get someone out here to claim the bodies right away. He led me back toward the house, through the woods, the trees protecting us from the rain. He avoided the area where I'd stumbled over Priscilla and I guessed that he had found her body, as well.

We were almost to the house when a series of neighs came from the barns.

"Valentine!" Damian said, suddenly running in that direction.

Sensing his panic—I knew he feared for the pregnant mare—I followed as fast as I could and prayed that everything would be all right. The last thing Damian needed was another disaster on his hands.

When I burst into the barn, he was already standing outside the stall. Tension had oozed out of his body, and he leaned his weight on the door, his attention focused through the opening at what was inside.

My own panic subsided and I joined him to watch Valentine clean the birth sack off the wriggling foal.

"Thank goodness they're both all right!" I said with a sigh.

The dark thing I'd felt within me all night suddenly lifted from my being. The birth of a live foal…at last something to celebrate rather than to dread. The earth in balance. A life for a death. Or several.

I knew Damian and I would face another ordeal with the authorities. And I with Damian. I had to talk to him, to tell him the truth. He needed to know why I came to Graylord Pastures. And I chose now to tell him, before the authorities got it out of me.

The least I could do was prepare him.

"Damian, there's something I've been keeping from you. Dawn Reed was my foster sister and my best friend,"

I said, keeping my eyes focused on the mare and foal. "I knew she would never have eloped and disappeared on me. I came here to find out what happened to her."

"I sensed there was more to you than met the eye."

He sounded so…neutral. As if he didn't care one way or the other. I swallowed hard and looked at him, and still I couldn't tell how he felt about it.

"Yes, well, if you want me to go, I understand."

"So you want to go?" he countered.

"There's Nissa to consider." I prayed he would keep the girl's needs in mind. That he wouldn't make me leave at first light. "When she learns that her mother is dead…"

"So Nissa's your only concern?"

"Aren't *you* concerned about how your daughter will react to what's happened?"

"Of course I am. I'm all Nissa has left." His jaw tightened, and it took him a moment before adding, "Whatever you decide, I won't send her away to school."

What I decide? Did that mean he was leaving the decision to go or stay to me? My spirits lifted a bit. He wasn't condemning me for keeping that information secret, after all. And he wasn't abandoning his daughter to someone else's care.

"That's good—forgetting about boarding school," I said. "Nissa is going to need you more than ever."

"You really care about her."

"I love her."

I wanted to say more, but I couldn't. I looked back into the stall where the foal was struggling to stand. I had experienced death this day, but my night would end with the celebration of a new life.

Suddenly it hit me. "The foal's coat…it's pale."

"Gray, like his sire."

"Centaur?" Had that been why the foal had waited so long to be born? I wondered. Until his sire was at peace? "Odd how a new life can change one's outlook on life."

"Odd," Damian agreed, turning me to look at him. "Priscilla was pregnant when I married her."

"Damian, you don't have to tell me—"

"I think I do. She was pregnant, but not by me."

I absorbed that information. No wonder Nissa looked nothing like him. She certainly didn't look like her mother.

"Who, then?" He didn't answer. Only one name came to mind. "Theo? He couldn't have known…he would have used it against you."

"Priscilla did love Nissa in her way. I guess when she left me, she thought her child would be better off with me than with her or with Nissa's biological father."

Plus, he'd made it very lucrative for Priscilla to keep quiet, which put a new spin on why he'd paid her off to keep away from her daughter.

"Will you tell Nissa?"

"Never. Not willingly. As far as I'm concerned, Nissa is the child of my heart. She has been since the day she was born. That's never going to change. I'm the only real parent she's ever had. I had thought that someday…but she doesn't need to know that she's related to a murderer. That might destroy her."

My heart swelled. I couldn't love Damian more. My own father had left me because I'd been too much of a burden to him after my mother had died. But Damian had gone to great lengths, nearly bankrupting the estate in the process, to keep the girl he'd chosen to be his daughter. And now he vowed to protect her forever.

Damian cupped my cheek and tilted my face up to his. "Nissa is the only one I've ever really loved…until you, Chloe. My heart nearly stopped when I saw you out there near the bluffs with Theo. My daughter needs a woman in her life and I need one in mine. I was hoping that woman would be you."

In his life…

"You mean you want me to stay?"

"Forever," he said, kissing me. "I love you, Chloe Morgan. I can't live without you."

All my doubts gone, I melted inside and kissed him back with all the fervor in my being.

Forever with Damian might be just long enough.

Epilogue

Burying my best friend was one of the hardest things I've ever had to do, but I got through it with Damian and Nissa and Alex at my side. To her credit, though Damian had let her go, Mrs. Avery was there with her nephew. Jack Larson might have been an opportunist, but his appearance told me he'd had some feelings for Dawn.

The week was doubly stressful since we had to deal with the authorities, giving them statements that would help them wrap up the murders. Mrs. Avery helped there, too, corroborating the clandestine affair between Priscilla and Theo. If she knew that Theo was Nissa's biological father—and I suspected she did—she kept that information to herself. Mrs. Avery was nothing if not loyal. I was glad her nephew took her in.

Slowly, we rebuilt our lives.

When another monetary crisis came up a few weeks later, and Alex muttered, "If only we could find the Equine Diamonds," the truth hit me.

But before I said anything, I wanted to be certain, so I sought out Nissa in her room.

"I was wondering something," I said, going straight

to the fish tank. "Some of those pieces of gravel are pretty big." And now that I looked at them, examined their crude shape, my heart began to race. "Where did they come from?"

"The attic," Nissa said, snuggling next to me and peering into the tank. Though she was still grief stricken over her mother, she'd drawn even closer to me than before. "There's a great old desk up there. It has all kinds of secret compartments. I found this old purple velvet bag filled with those rocks."

Rocks?

The Equine Diamonds had been right under our noses all along!

Nissa hadn't realized their worth because they remained uncut. They didn't have facets like the stones in her mother's jewelry box.

My announcement first caused disbelief in Damian and Alex, and then when I produced the proof, celebration.

After selling most of the diamonds, Damian was able to clear the farm of debt and to give his brother enough money to start over wherever he wanted to go. Alex didn't go far. He bought his own place down the road but chose to continue working at Graylord Pastures, at least for the time being. I figured he was a forever kind of person, also, as long as he had the option to do whatever it was he wanted.

Damian had the largest of the Equine Diamonds cut and mounted in a band of two gold horses. He gave me the stunning engagement ring for my birthday. We'll be married on Christmas Eve.

For me life turned out better than I ever imagined. Soon I would have a husband and a daughter who both loved me and hopefully another child would soon be on the way. I am truly blessed to know in my heart that I will never again feel abandoned.

When I think of Dawn, as I often do, it is not without sadness, but then I close my eyes and hear her laughter and picture her and Centaur racing through Graylord Pastures....

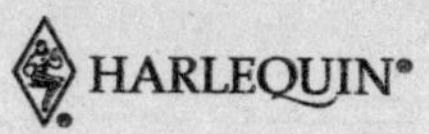

INTRIGUE®

As the summer comes to a close, things really begin to heat up as Harlequin Intrigue presents...

Big Sky Bounty Hunters: No man's a match for these Montana tough guys...but a woman's another story.

Don't miss this brand-new series from some of your favorite authors!

GOING TO EXTREMES
BY AMANDA STEVENS
August 2005

BULLSEYE
BY JESSICA ANDERSEN
September 2005

WARRIOR SPIRIT
BY CASSIE MILES
October 2005

FORBIDDEN CAPTOR
BY JULIE MILLER
November 2005

RILEY'S RETRIBUTION
BY RUTH GLICK,
writing as Rebecca York
December 2005

Available at your favorite retail outlet.

www.eHarlequin.com

HIBSBH